THE CASTLE MADE FOR LOVE

Yolande's desperation knew no bounds.

Up until now her life was as perfect as any princess in a storybook. A landed countess, blessed with beauty, intelligence and wealth, she lived in a magnificent castle on the edge of a dark, mysterious forest.

But the fairy tale abruptly became a nightmare when she was promised in marriage to the Marquis de Montereau. Yolande had heard a great deal about the Marquis: he was the most notorious rake in all Paris. He might be willing to marry her for her estates, but he would never love her.

Knowing she would rather die than wed a man she hardly knew and certainly despised, Yolande saw only one way to appraise her future bridegroom and resign herself to marriage.

She would go to Paris impersonating a woman of less than perfect virtue. She would force the Marquis to love her as a woman—not as the owner of a priceless castle.

BARBARA CARTLAND

Bantam Books by Barbara Cartland
Ask your bookseller for the books you have missed

1 The Daring Deception
4 Lessons in Love
6 The Bored Bridegroom
8 The Dangerous Dandy
9 The Ruthless Rake
10 The Wicked Marquis
11 The Castle of Fear
14 The Karma of Love
18 The Frightened Bride
19 The Shadow of Sin
21 The Tears of Love
22 A Very Naughty Angel
23 Call of the Heart
24 The Devil in Love
25 As Eagles Fly
27 Say Yes, Samantha
28 The Cruel Count
29 The Mask of Love
30 Fire on the Snow
31 An Arrow of Love
33 A Kiss for the King
34 A Frame of Dreams
35 The Fragrant Flower
36 The Elusive Earl
38 The Golden Illusion
41 Passions in the Sand
43 An Angel in Hell
44 The Wild Cry of Love
45 The Blue-Eyed Witch
46 The Incredible Honeymoon
47 A Dream from the Night
48 Conquered by Love
49 Never Laugh at Love
50 The Secret of the Glen
51 The Proud Princess
52 Hungry for Love
53 The Heart Triumphant
54 The Dream and the Glory
55 The Taming of Lady Lorinda
56 The Disgraceful Duke
57 Vote for Love
59 The Magic of Love
60 Kiss the Moonlight
61 A Rhapsody of Love
62 The Marquis Who Hated Women
63 Look, Listen and Love
64 A Duel with Destiny
65 The Curse of the Clan
66 Punishment of a Vixen
67 The Outrageous Lady
68 A Touch of Love
69 The Dragon and the Pearl
70 The Love Pirate
71 The Temptation of Torilla
72 Love and the Loathsome Leopard
73 The Naked Battle
74 The Hellcat and the King
75 No Escape from Love
76 The Castle Made for Love
77 The Sign of Love

Barbara Cartland's Library of Love

1 The Sheik
2 His Hour
3 The Knave of Diamonds
4 A Safety Match
5 The Hundredth Chance
6 The Reason Why
7 The Way of an Eagle
8 The Vicissitudes of Evangeline
9 The Bars of Iron
10 Man and Maid
11 The Sons of the Sheik

Barbara Cartland

The Castle Made for Love

THE CASTLE MADE FOR LOVE

A Bantam Book / December 1977

ISBN 0-553-11580-4

Published simultaneously in the United States and Canada

Bantam Books are published by Bantam Books, Inc. Its trademark, consisting of the words "Bantam Books" and the portrayal of a bantam, is registered in the United States Patent Office and in other countries. Marca Registrada. Bantam Books, Inc., 666 Fifth Avenue, New York, New York 10019.

PRINTED IN THE UNITED STATES OF AMERICA

Author's Note

The Castle "made for love" in this story is the Castle of Usse, built on the edge of the dark, mysterious forest of Chinon in the Indre Valley.

It inspired Perrault to write the tale *The Sleeping Beauty*. Built in the sixteenth and seventeenth centuries, it is the most beautiful fairy-tale building I have ever seen.

The Paris International Exhibition of 1867 was the apotheosis of the Second Empire. Held mainly for political reasons, it attracted visitors from all over the world and the list of Royal guests was endless.

The whole of France became intoxicated with pleasure and pride—pride in its machinery and magnificent Army, pleasure in its money and its beautiful Capital.

But three years later the Prussians had defeated the French Army at Sedan, the Emperor Louis Napoleon and the Empress Eugénie had fled into exile, the Palace of the Tuileries was burnt down, and the Siege of Paris began.

Chapter One

1867

Mademoiselle la Comtesse Marie Teresa Madeleine de Beauharnais stood on the terrace and looked out over the green land which sloped towards the River Indre.

"Mine! All mine!" she said to herself.

Then she turned round to lean against the stone balustrade and look up at the Castle behind her.

Built on a cliff where the forest of Chinon ended, the Castle stood above flowered terraces.

Its massive fortified towers, and its turrets, dormer windows, and chimneys, were silhouetted against the green background, and with the whole structure picked out in white stone it appeared to have stepped straight out of a fairy-tale.

Looking at it now, she expected to see Knights in armour with their pennants, flags, and fine horses riding out to fight with their lances against the dragons that lurked in the forests, or the evil which attacked good.

She remembered that when she was a child her father told her stories of such Knights and how the Castle in which they lived was redolent with the history of France.

To think of her father made her expect to see

him come through one of the arched doorways and call out to her as he invariably did when he returned home.

"Yola! Yola!"

No-one else called her by that special name.

Her father had wished her to be christened Yolande, which was the name of one of their most illustrious ancestors, but her mother predictably had insisted that every name she bore must be that of a Saint.

"Yola! Yola!"

She could hear his voice now, echoing up to the Beauharnais flag which flew above the innumerable roofs and which could be seen for miles round by those who served them or lived on the estate.

But now her father was dead, and because there was no son, Yola had inherited the Castle.

For a moment her pride of possession left her and she felt very small and lonely as she thought how much responsibility rested upon her shoulders.

How could she manage without her father?

How would anything seem the same without his laughter, without the talks they enjoyed together and the times they had ridden over the estate, glorying in the beauty of the Loire Valley?

It was her father who had told her how privileged they were to live in what was called "the Garden of France."

It was not only the beauty of it and its mild, soft atmosphere, but the magic which made all who lived there different from the inhabitants of any other part of France.

Yola had grown up not only with the tales of Knightly valour but also with the legends of Joan of Arc.

She had made her father tell her over and over again how Joan had appeared and visited the Dauphin at the Castle of Chinon.

While waiting to be received by him, she had spent two days fasting and praying at an Inn not far from the town.

Although her mystical "voices" had told her that the Dauphin must throw out the hated British Conquerors, the Courtiers had laughed at the idea that a peasant-girl could be anything but an imposter.

When finally she was admitted to the Palace, the Great Hall was lit with fifty torches and three hundred gentlemen in rich apparel were assembled there.

To test her, the Dauphin hid amongst the crowd and a Courtier wore his robes.

Joan had advanced shyly, then immediately recognising the future King she went straight to him.

She knelt and embraced his knees.

"Gentle Dauphin," she said, "my name is Joan the Maid. The King of Heaven sent word by me that you will be anointed and crowned in the City of Rheims and you will be lieutenant to the King of Heaven."

Charles, however, was hesitant.

He had always doubted whether Charles VI was really his father, because his mother, Isabella of Bavaria, was notoriously immoral and had had innumerable lovers.

Then Joan said to him:

"I tell you in the name of Our Lord Christ that you are the heir to the throne of France and a true son of the King."

It was all so dramatic, Yola thought, and now because Joan of Arc seemed so real to her, she prayed for courage that she might not be afraid but should rule in a small way as Charles had been able to do once he had been crowned King.

Then, as if the seriousness of her thoughts amused her, she shook herself free of them and turned again to look out towards the Indre.

It was so wonderful, she thought, to be home after spending a year in a school near Paris since her father had died.

She had not been able to return to the Castle because there had been no-one to chaperon her, but now that she was eighteen her grandmother had left her Villa where she lived at Nice to come to Beauharnais.

It was the beginning of May and the creepers climbing over the terraces in front of the Castle were coming into bud.

The purple-flowered wistaria was a poem of beauty, while the daffodils, hyacinths, narcissus, cyclamen, and anemones made the garden a kaleidoscope of colour.

The camelias were pink and white against the Castle walls, and in the valley the blossoms on the fruit trees turned it into a fairy-land.

As Yola walked across the court-yard to the stone steps which led up to the great entrance doors, she looked like a flower herself in the soft pink of her small crinoline.

It was, of course, *Monsieur* Worth who in the year of the great Paris International Exhibition had changed the fashion by decreeing that the huge crinoline which had been made the vogue by the Empress Eugénie should be replaced by a much smaller and shorter one.

The petite crinoline had become the rage almost overnight. Gowns were still, however, worn over small hoops and there was a mass of draperies, ruchings, and trimmings.

It meant of course that seamstresses must work every hour of the clock and that the astronomical sum of sixteen hundred francs was charged for even a simple little costume in the new shape.

Yola had bought a few gowns in which to return home and had been astounded at the prices she was asked to pay for them.

Hats which were nothing bigger than a small bowl perched on top of an elaborate coiffure of plaits and curls cost one hundred twenty francs, and she told herself that it was wrong that so much should be spent on mere feminine ornamentation.

But she knew that none of the pleasure-seeking, wildly extravagant Parisians would be likely to listen to such a revolutionary idea as economy.

Yola had, however, purchased what she needed carefully and sparingly.

She knew that now that her father was dead she was exceedingly rich, but she was wise enough to tell herself that she must decide first how she intended to live before she expended large sums on gowns which she might not need once she returned home.

She felt sure, however, that her grandmother, who was worldly-wise, would want her to spend some time in Paris so that she could be introduced to Society and doubtless attend State functions at the Tuileries Palace.

Not that aristocrats of the old régime like the Dowager *Comtesse* de Beauharnais approved of the Emperor and the Empress, whom they considered to be "up-starts."

But Yola felt certain that at the back of her grandmother's mind and those of her other relations would be the idea that she must meet eligible men, one of whom she would eventually marry.

'I shall be in no hurry,' she thought.

She stood still for a moment on top of the steps and looked again over the valley covered with blossoms.

'For the moment this is my Kingdom,' she added to herself, 'and I have no desire to share it with anyone.'

She went into the Castle, climbing the great seventeenth-century staircase to find her grandmother in the beautiful Salon whose windows also overlooked the valley.

There were bowls of hot-house flowers standing on the magnificent furniture which had been handed down for generations, and their fragrance filled the air.

Sitting in a high-backed chair which was covered with needle-work made and embroidered by a sixteenth-century ancestor, her grandmother looked like a painting by Boucher.

With her white hair piled high on her head and

the long fingers of her blue-veined hands glittering with rings, it would have been impossible, Yola thought, not to recognise that she was an aristocrat.

"Where have you been, *ma chérie*?" the *Comtesse* asked.

"I have been out on the terrace, *Grandmère*," Yola replied, "and I decided that this is without exception the most wonderful Castle in the whole of the Loire Valley."

"You are just like your father," her grandmother said with a smile. "He always said that while Chinon and Blois were magnificent, and Chambord and Chenonceaux beautiful, our Castle had a magical, mystical quality that was different from everyone else's."

"That is exactly what I feel, *Grandmère*," Yola said. "It is what I believed as a child to be a fairy-tale Castle come true."

"And that is why," her grandmother said, "we must find you a Prince Charming so that there shall be a happy ending to your story."

Yola stiffened.

"There is no hurry for that, *Grandmère*."

"But there is," her grandmother insisted, "you see, *ma petite*, though I am very happy to be here with you, I came against my Doctor's instructions and I cannot stay long."

"*Grandmère*, it is almost as warm here as it is in Nice, and you know as well as I do that many of the trees in the gardens are semi-tropical. Why, we even have some palm trees, and Papa has grown shrubs and orchids which in the past could only be found near the Mediterranean."

Even as she spoke Yola knew that her grandmother was not really attending.

"You know, of course, my child," she said, "what your father wished for you?"

"With . . . regard to . . . marriage?" Yola asked hesitantly.

"He must have spoken of it?"

"No, *Grandmère*, we talked of almost everything,

but he never actually mentioned any man in particular whom he would wish me to marry."

"Well, fortunately, I saw your father only a month before he died," the *Comtesse* said. "He came to stay with me at Nice before he went to Venice, an ill-omened visit which he should never have made."

There was a sharpness now in the *Comtesse*'s voice, but Yola said nothing.

She knew only too well why her father had gone to Venice; but it was something she did not wish to discuss with her grandmother, knowing what her feelings would be.

"Your father talked to me about your future," the *Comtesse* went on. "Perhaps he had a presentiment that he would not live very long, or perhaps he thought you were growing up and would soon be old enough to be betrothed."

Yola moved restlessly across the room.

The sunshine coming through the windows revealed the blue lights in her dark hair and the exquisite purity of her white skin.

As she stood against one of the dark velvet curtains, looking out with unseeing eyes, she looked very lovely and her grandmother paused for a moment to appreciate the picture she made. Then she said:

"I suppose the reason why your father did not mention whom he wished you to marry was that it had been so long in his thoughts and in mine that he thought you must be aware of it."

"Whom are you talking about, *Grandmère*?" Yola asked.

Now she walked back from the window to stand at her grandmother's side.

"The Marquis de Montereau, of course!"

For a moment Yola stared at her grandmother incredulously. Then she said in a voice that seemed almost to be strangled in her throat:

"The Marquis de Montereau!"

"Yes, *ma chérie*," her grandmother said. "You

must have heard of him since you were a child, although you may not have seen him. He is not only a distant cousin, but he lived here until he was twelve. Let me see—you must only have been three at the time, so it is not surprising that you do not remember him—unless he has stayed here since?"

"No, *Grandmère*, he has not stayed here since I can remember."

"That was, of course, due to your mother," the *Comtesse* said, "but then . . ."

She checked herself as if she thought that nothing good would come of disparaging the dead.

Yola was well aware of the words that were left unsaid.

Her mother, contrary to every tradition of the family, refused to have anyone to stay with them.

It was to be expected that the *Comte* de Beauharnais, as the head of a large and ancient family, would not only provide for his less fortunate relatives but also house a number of them.

When he had inherited from his father, the Castle had been filled with cousins, aunts, great-aunts, grandparents, and close friends, all of whom had grown old beside the owner.

But her mother had managed within five years of their marriage to disperse them all.

What was more, she would not open the house to friends who for years past had come from Paris to spend some weeks or a month in the Castle which they admired and loved.

Yola could remember when she was a child endless arguments and rows between her father and mother because her father wished to entertain and her mother was adamant that they should not do so.

Then suddenly her father had given up the battle and accepted that the guest-rooms in the Castle should be closed, and that his hospitable impulses which were so much a part of his character should be curbed.

The Castle had seemed very large and quiet and sometimes grim as she grew up.

If there had not been her father to laugh with, if they had not escaped to go riding so that they could feel free and unrestrained, Yola felt it would have been intolerable.

Gradually she began to understand and realised that her mother ought never to have been married.

She had really wished to become a nun, but her parents appreciated that the *Comte* de Beauharnais with his magnificent Castle and great estates was an important and highly eligible *parti*.

They had forced her against her will to accept the arrangements they had made, without consulting either her or, as Yola knew, her father.

He had accepted as inevitable that his marriage would be an arranged one and that his bride would bring him a huge dowry to add to the already large fortune he possessed.

Only when he realised the violence of his wife's hatred for him did he know with horror that he was sentenced to a lifetime of misery.

They had had one child, after which there was no chance of there being any more.

Yola could never remember her mother kissing her with any affection or holding her in her arms. Her days and many of her nights had been spent in the exquisitely beautiful Chapel which stood alone a little way from the house.

Built between 1520 and 1530, it was in the purest Renaissance style and connoisseurs went into ecstasies over its sculpture and decoration.

But to Yola it was a place of repentance which vibrated with the wrath of God and the fear of punishment.

Forced to attend a Church Service every day before she could read or understand what was being said, her only consolation had been that sitting in the hard, carved pew she could look at a magnificent Aubusson tapestry which traced the history of Joan of Arc.

It was thus that the Saint was impressed indelibly

on her mind, while her mother's religion made her feel cold and critical.

How could it be right for her mother to wish to be a Saint, to pray incessantly to God and at the same time to be so unkind, unsympathetic, and unfeeling towards her husband?

Why should she expect God to bless her, when she in her turn gave to other people only hatred or indifference?

It was a long time before Yola put such thoughts into words, and yet they were there as soon as she could begin to think objectively.

It was not surprising that her father was everything in her life, and because he was an extremely intelligent, well-read man he not only taught her but talked to her as if she were a contemporary.

She could argue on abstract subjects almost before she could do simple arithmetic.

She read the French Classics when other children were learning nursery-rhymes, and her father also taught her to appreciate beauty while his suffering made her sensitive and perceptive about everybody and everything.

Looking at her granddaughter now, the *Comtesse* thought that her huge dark eyes mirrored her feelings so clearly that anyone watching her could actually see what she was thinking.

Aloud she asked:

"What do you know of the Marquis if you have never met him?"

"I have . . . heard of . . . him," Yola replied.

"From whom?"

"The girls at school. He was talked about by them, and presumably by their parents, as often as they discussed the Emperor."

The *Comtesse*'s lips tightened.

She might live in a secluded Villa in the South of France, but she was well aware that the Emperor Louis Napoleon's love-affairs were discussed over the length and breadth of France, and none of them to his credit.

"The Marquis is a young man," she said after a moment, "and must therefore be expected to enjoy himself."

"Yes, of course, *Grandmère*," Yola agreed, "but I do not think that the pleasures of Paris will give him an appreciation of the Castle."

"How can you be sure of that?" the *Comtesse* queried almost sharply. "He was happy here as a boy. Your grandfather was very fond of him and so was I."

She was silent for a moment. Then as if she looked back into the past she said slowly:

"He was a handsome little boy, and his tutors spoke well of him. I remember your grandfather used to take him riding and say that he was fearless on a horse."

"I am sure he is a sportsman," Yola said, "but that is not to say, *Grandmère*, that he is the kind of man I want to marry."

Her grandmother made a gesture with one of her hands and her rings glittered.

"My dear child," she said softly, "the decision does not rest with you."

"That is not true!"

"Not true?"

There was no doubt that the *Comtesse* was startled.

"I intend to choose my own husband."

"But that is impossible!" her grandmother cried. "No French *jeune fille* has such a choice. Of course, if you loathe the Marquis on sight and he hates you, then excuses could be made and negotiations, even if they were already started, could be stopped, and we could find someone else."

"We?" Yola questioned.

"It is just a figure of speech," her grandmother said with a smile. "As your father left everything in my hands, I have written to the Marquis—Leonide, as I used to call him—to ask him to stay with us next month."

"You have already written to him?" Yola questioned.

"I have not of course said anything specific or binding," her grandmother replied quickly, "but the Marquis is a man of the world. He will read between the lines, and I have a feeling that he was waiting to hear from me."

"Why should you think that?"

"I gathered from your father—of course, as I did not know he was going to die, I did not press him for details—that there was already an understanding between him and the Marquis that when you were old enough you should be affianced."

"I do not believe that Papa would have forced me into a marriage without first consulting me."

Yola's voice was firm and there was a note of rebellion in it which her grandmother did not miss.

"I am sure, *ma petite*, he would have discussed it with you. I know how much you meant to each other, and your father would never have made you unhappy."

"It will make me very unhappy," Yola said, "to be married off to a man of whom I know nothing. You said yourself, *Grandmère*, that you have not seen him since he was twelve. How do you know what he is like now?"

Her grandmother was silent and Yola went on:

"The girls at school talked of him as if he were Don Juan, Casanova, and the Devil himself all rolled into one."

"Oh, no! That is not true!" her grandmother cried.

"They said it was true," Yola replied. "I used to get tired of hearing of the exploits of the Marquis just as I was sick of hearing of the different ladies who were favoured by the Emperor."

"There is no comparison between the two," the *Comtesse* said swiftly. "Louis Napoleon may be Emperor of France but he is not a man I would welcome here. The Marquis's family is as good as our own and he has Beauharnais blood in his veins."

She paused to look a little apprehensively at

the darkness in her granddaughter's eyes before she went on:

"Of course you know that Montereau Castle was destroyed by the Revolutionaries and their estates confiscated, while we here were so fortunate."

Just for a moment Yola's expression softened.

She had always been touched by the fact that during the French Revolution when Anjou was one of the chief battlegrounds of the Republicans and Royalists, General Santerre had arrived from Paris with a troop of Revolutionary reinforcements.

Then miraculously the beauty and the atmosphere of the Garden of France had cooled their ardour so that they had laid down their muskets and cast off their accoutrements.

That was why so many Castles in the Loire Valley had not been destroyed or burnt and the families who owned them had not lost their lives.

"So you are thinking," Yola said slowly, "that the Marquis has been waiting unmarried all these years to own Beauharnais?"

"It is what your father wished," the *Comtesse* replied, "and you have to marry someone."

"Why in such a hurry?" Yola enquired. "I have only just left school. I have seen nothing of the world, and I thought, *Grandmère*, that at least I would have a Season in Paris."

"Paris is now nothing but a sink of iniquity!" the *Comtesse* exclaimed harshly. "The Emperor and Empress reign over a régime of such extravagance and such depravity that they have scandalised every decent country in Europe."

Yola looked startled.

"Do you really believe that is true?"

"It is true," the *Comtesse* said grimly, "and this International Exhibition that is taking place this year is only a ruse of the Emperor to cover up, from the eyes of the world his deficiencies in other respects."

While her grandmother spoke so positively Yola was silent.

It would have been impossible for the pupils at the fashionable finishing-school at St. Cloud not to be aware of a great deal of what took place in Paris.

Girls, who were supposed to be blind and deaf until they emerged from the School-Room into the Salon, heard and repeated every item of gossip that was exchanged between their parents, their parents' friends, and of course the servants.

Her father had often said, Yola remembered, that people always behaved as if the servants had no feelings and the children were morons.

"They talk over their heads as if they did not exist," he said, "and yet I am convinced that more scandal is carried from house to house by the Major-Domos and Grooms-of-Chambers than actually travels from Salon to Salon."

Yola had often visited the other pupils in their homes and she found that the parents talked to each other when their daughters were present in a manner which they would have thought twice about in the presence of their friends.

And many things which were said concerned the Marquis de Montereau.

"What has *le Marquis Méchant* been up to now?" Yola heard one attractive Parisian say to her husband when she and their daughter were supposedly looking at photograph albums in the Salon.

"What do you imagine?" had been the reply. "And it will mean another duel, another *affaire scandaleuse,* and one can only hope to Heaven that the newspapers do not get hold of it."

"He is incorrigible!" the lady of the house had exclaimed.

It was not a censorious criticism, but almost one of delight.

Thinking of it now, Yola realised that if she married the Marquis de Montereau as her grandmother wished, she would not have a marriage of frustration and privation like her father's, but one of endless frivolity, extravagance, and scandal!

Something hard and resolute rose within her to

make her feel that she must fight every inch of the way to prevent herself from being swept up the aisle with such a man.

It was inconceivable that her father, who had loved her, should wish her to embark on a life which would obviously be one of unhappiness.

For how could she keep up with the sophisticated society in which the Marquis moved?

She was sure that he was almost a ring-leader of those in the pleasure-seeking Capital who sought amusement twenty-four hours a day and had no time for anything else.

She remembered reading, in one of the newspapers which the Headmistress of her school would not have approved of the girls perusing, a review of the Season written by an obviously exhausted critic:

> *We are in a Parisian Paradise, or a Parisian Hell. Every night since January first has been spent in festivals, spectacles, concerts, and dances. It is a perpetual coming-and-going, a constant to-ing and fro-ing, an unending treadmill.*

'Is that what I want of life?' Yola now asked herself, and she knew the answer was a very forceful 'No!'

Aloud she said:

"I wish, *Grandmère,* that you had asked me before you wrote to the Marquis. I thought it would be pleasant to have a quiet time before we started to entertain."

She smiled to make her words seem less censorious. Then she went on:

"I want to renew my acquaintance with our employees on the estate, to visit the farms, to find out what has been done in the fields and in the gardens. It will all take time."

"You have a month, *ma chérie,*" her grandmother replied. "I have invited the Marquis for the beginning of June."

Yola pressed her lips together to prevent herself from retorting that the Castle was hers and she would entertain when and whom she wished.

Then she knew that she could not be unkind or cross with her grandmother, whom she loved.

She rose, bent down, and kissed the elderly woman's soft cheek before she said:

"When we hear from the Marquis, *Grandmère*, I think it would be an excellent idea if we invite some other eligible bachelors to meet several of my friends with whom I went to school. It would then not be so obvious why he has been summoned to Beauharnais."

She knew by the startled expression in her grandmother's eyes that although her letter had been very discreet it had in fact made it very clear that the invitation was not just for pleasure.

'I have no intention of marrying him,' Yola thought to herself.

At the same time, she knew it was going to be very difficult to circumvent her grandmother's plans, especially as she obviously intended to keep reiterating that it had been her father's wish.

Leaving the Salon, Yola walked through the long stone corridors to the room which had been particularly her father's.

Her mother had hardly ever entered it, and it was here that he had sat with his daughter, often talking late into the night.

The walls were lined with the books from which he had taught her, and there were just two of their favourite pictures on the walls that had been taken from other parts of the Castle.

It was a large and beautiful room and had been used by the reigning *Comtes* since the sixteenth century.

It was here that the Knights in ancient days had held their Councils of War, and Yola felt it was a suitable place for her to plan her own campaign.

"It is going to be a hard battle," she said aloud, as if talking to her father.

She shut the door behind her and walked across the room to the large desk at which he had always sat.

Yola settled herself in the high-back red velvet chair which was embroidered with the Beauharnais coat-of-arms.

Then she looked down at the blotter her father had used, at the great silver ink-pot that had been in the family for three hundred years, and at all the other things which littered the desk and which were particularly his own.

Quite suddenly it seemed to Yola impossible that he was no longer with her and she was alone.

Because she was a woman, her grandmother and the rest of the family would force her into marriage as quickly as possible so that she would have a man to dominate her, to force her to do as he wished.

"How could you have died before I grew up, Papa?" Yola asked.

She remembered how they had so often talked of the things they would do together.

"I will take you to Balls," her father had said, "and I know, my dearest, you will be the most beautiful person in the room."

She had laughed at him.

"You are flattering me, Papa!—something you have always said you would never do."

"I am appraising you as I might a stranger," her father answered, "and I am not being prejudiced when I tell you you are very different from the other girls of your age."

"Why do you think that?" Yola asked, eager for him to praise her.

"It is not just that you are beautiful. There have been beautiful women in the Beauharnais family for generations," her father said slowly, "and it is not because you are instinctively graceful and walk as if your feet hardly touch the ground."

He paused before he added:

"It is, Yola, *ma petite*, something very different."

"Then what is it?"

"It is difficult to put into words," her father replied. "Perhaps because I wanted a child so desperately, because I beseeched Heaven to send me one who would embody all my ideals, you seem to me to be a gift from God."

He spoke very seriously and Yola looked at him wide-eyed.

"Do you . . . really mean . . . that, Papa?" she asked in a low voice.

"I mean it because it is true," the *Comte* answered. "It is what you think and feel inside, my dearest, which shines through you like a light and which makes you beautiful beyond the conventional meaning of the word."

Yola put her arms round his neck and pressed her cheek close against his.

"I want to be everything you want me to be," she said, "but you will have to help me, Papa."

"That is what I have tried to do ever since you were born," he said. "I love your mind, Yola, for it makes everything you say sharp, clear, and logical, which is very different from the usual scatter-brained feminine observations."

Yola smiled.

"You are being very scathing and critical."

"I am saying what I think," he replied; then he went on: "And I respect your courage."

"Which I have inherited from you."

"Before you were born, I wished you to be a son," the *Comte* said, "but now I am very content with my daughter. You are original, inventive, and you have a mental and physical bravery that is worthy of a man."

"And who could ask for higher praise?" Yola asked almost mockingly. "I wish I had been a boy for your sake, Papa. At the same time, I cannot help feeling that it might be rather amusing to be a woman if in fact I have all the qualities with which you credit me."

"Amusing for you, but undoubtedly painful for those who love you," the *Comte* said quietly.

"Painful?" Yola questioned.

"Many men will love you," the *Comte* replied, "and I suppose I shall be very jealous of them. But because I think you are like me, you will love only one person in your life with all your heart and soul."

Yola had hardly understood what he meant at the time, but now his words came back to her.

She knew that if she married the Marquis or anyone else without loving him with all her heart and soul, her marriage would be one of misery and despair as her father's had been.

'How can *Grandmère* expect me to accept the Marquis, knowing what I have heard about him?' she asked herself.

Then she knew that while her grandmother might be determined to return as quickly as she could to the South of France, she was at the same time behaving in an entirely normal and correct manner in marrying Yola off as soon as possible.

It was exactly what any other Frenchwoman in the same position would do automatically.

She had a rich, eligible, attractive granddaughter, and the only surprise lay in the fact that she was prepared to accept a mere Marquis as Yola's husband and the future owner of the Castle.

She might have looked higher amongst the Bourbon Princes who still existed despite the Revolution.

"To marry the Marquis de Montereau is impossible!" Yola said.

Everything she had ever heard about him seemed to be repeated and repeated in her mind.

She knew that he typified the *jeunesse dorée* of French Society, and thinking back she was quite certain he also shone in the world of the Courtesans.

A French *jeune fille* was expected to be very innocent and to have no knowledge of the women who embellished Paris like beautiful, exotic, and extremely expensive flowers.

But Yola would have been very stupid if she had not realised that there were two Social Circles in Paris which intermingled in a manner which would not have been permitted in any other country in Europe.

There was the Imperial family headed by Napoleon III, who was married to the Empress Eugénie, the beautiful Spaniard whom the French suspected of urging her husband continually towards war.

Yola had heard that life at the Tuileries Palace was dull and bourgeois and laughed at by the real French aristocrats who wished to disparage everything about Louis Napoleon Bonaparte.

But in his endless pursuit of beautiful women the Emperor gave them every ground for criticism.

He was closely followed by other members of the Imperial family: Prince Napoleon, first cousin of the Emperor, was one of the most gifted yet controversial and significant figures in the Second Empire.

When Yola was young he had become an Imperial Highness and a Senator, and her father had read her his speeches which showed him to be a champion of democracy.

But when she was at school, the Prince's private life was the subject of girlish giggles and much whispering in corners.

She learnt that like the Emperor his mistresses were legion. A father of one of her friends, not realising that she was listening, had said:

"I called on Prince Napoleon this morning. I had heard there was always a petticoat left trailing in his private apartments—this morning there were two!"

Indivisibly in her mind the Prince was linked with the Marquis and she was sure that they were each as bad as the other.

It was these two men and the Emperor who had allowed the *demi-mondaines* to encroach on the Social World.

In her grandmother's time no Lady of Quality and certainly no young girl would have known that such creatures even existed.

But the girls at school had whispered names which

at first meant nothing to Yola, and yet she heard them repeated again and again.

It had been impossible for her not to wonder who these ladies were who apparently filled the Bois with their smart horses and *chic* appearance and gave parties which were reported in the newspapers as if they were Roman orgies.

It all seemed very strange, and Yola had longed this last year for her father to be there to explain to her what it all meant.

But he was dead and all she could think of now was that every newspaper story had contained the name of the Marquis.

If she read of a party, first night at the Theatre, a Reception, or a fancy-dress Ball, the Marquis's name always featured prominently amongst the guests.

He was as much written about and certainly as much talked about as the Emperor and the Prince Napoleon.

His idiosyncrasies and his scandals were spoken of in the same hushed tones as were used when speaking of people like *Madame* Musard, who owed her vast wealth to the King of the Netherlands and who gave fantastic parties, or the *Princesse* de Castiglione, who apparently, Yola learnt, was loved to distraction by the Emperor.

It was all very hard to understand, but one thing was certain, one thing was unmistakable: whatever happened in Paris, the Marquis was part of it.

"I will not marry him, Papa," she said aloud, with her hands on her father's desk. "You cannot have known what he is like."

She waited almost as if she expected her father to argue with her as he had done so often.

Sometimes it had been a duel of wits and she thought their words clashed through the air like rapiers.

They fenced and thrust at each other, usually to

end up laughing, with Yola putting her arms round her father's neck to cry:

"I won! Tell me I won, Papa! I do so long to beat you!"

"You have won, my dearest," he would say, but his eyes would be twinkling.

She had invariably had the feeling that had he wished he would have defeated her all too easily.

Yet it had all been such fun, so exciting and stimulating that when he had died she felt crippled without him as if she had lost an arm or a leg.

Now, at the most important moment of her life, when she stood, as it were, at the cross-roads, there was no-one to help her to make the decision which would decide the future.

"Look at it this way, Papa," she said as if he were sitting opposite her, "I am young, and you have given me noble ideals to believe in, to fight for and try to achieve."

Her voice rang out as she asked:

"Do you really believe that someone like the Marquis would help me develop the estates as we planned we would do? Would be able to make the Castle a place where people with intelligence and brains would wish to congregate?"

Yola paused before she went on slowly:

"You used to say that when I was grown up we would have a Salon not in Paris but in the country, here in the Garden of France, which is so beautiful and so conducive to thought."

She threw out her hands in an expressive gesture as she asked:

"Do you really believe that would amuse the Marquis?"

Again she paused before she continued:

"He goes from *boudoir* to *boudoir*. He is talked about with one woman this week, another the next, a third the week after that. He is seen at the Races, in the Bois, at the State Balls and parties given by actresses and Courtesans."

She gave a little laugh which had no humour in it.

"You always said, Papa, that a man could not think in such circumstances, and I am sure that is true."

She sighed.

"I want to live as you and I decided we would, through our minds, so that we can see beneath the surface and find what you called the World behind the World. That is the way to develop, and that, ultimately, is the way to help France."

There was almost a note of ecstasy in Yola's voice.

Then as if she realised there was no-one to answer her, she put her hands up over her eyes.

"Help me, Papa. Tell me what to do," she begged, "for to be truthful . . . I am frightened . . . frightened of what will . . . become of me."

She did not cry although the tears pricked her eyes.

Then as if she listened and heard only the silence, she resolutely sat back in the chair, and as if to divert her mind from the intensity of her feelings she opened the drawer in front of her.

It was filled with papers and she thought vaguely that she must go through them because she supposed they concerned the estate.

She must learn, she thought, every detail that her father had accumulated about it.

Then she closed the drawer and looked in another. Here there were a number of maps and plans, and she knew these were important and she must study them when she had the time.

She opened a third drawer.

When she saw what it contained she was very still.

Slowly, almost reluctantly, she lifted the miniature which lay on top of a pile of letters and looked at it.

It depicted a woman.

She was not very young and not strictly and

classically beautiful. But there was something compelling and very attractive about her eyes and the faint smile of amusement which curved her lips.

Her dark hair was swept back from an intelligent forehead, and she wore round her neck a locket on a green velvet ribbon.

Yola sat looking at the miniature for a long time, until just as if her father had spoken to her she knew what she must do.

For a moment it seemed too extraordinary, almost too fantastic to contemplate, and yet the idea was so clear, so distinct, that it was impossible not to know it might be the solution to her problem.

Very gently she replaced the miniature where it had lain, then she closed the drawer and locked it.

As she put the key in the middle drawer where the servants were unlikely to find it, she looked across the room and said very quietly beneath her breath:

"Thank you . . . Papa!"

Chapter Two

Yola drove the chaise which had always been her father's favourite conveyance with two horses pulling it towards the small town of Langeais.

It was where they shopped from Beauharnais, and there was also in the town a fifteenth-century Castle which had been built on the site of an early fortress.

Her father had been friends with the owner of it, but Yola was not today calling at the Castle since she had plans which she had lain awake last night perfecting in her mind.

Accompanying her was the middle-aged groom who was in charge of the stables at Beauharnais and whom Yola had known since she was a child.

He had been delighted when she came home, and as soon as they started driving through the lush green countryside he talked of the horses she must ride and one in particular which he hoped she would break in.

Yola made the expected answers and responded to his enthusiasm, but part of her mind was elsewhere.

When they had crossed the River Loire and reached the town, she drove through the traffic of wagons, country-carts, and a few prosperous-looking carriages to draw up at the Pharmacy.

Holding her horses steady, she took two pieces of paper from the pocket of her short jacket.

"Will you have this made up, Jacques," she asked. "It will take I think about fifteen or twenty minutes, and while you are waiting here is a list of some other things I require."

There were quite a number of them, silks for embroidery, needles, cottons, yards of tape, and various other small items, which Jacques looked at with consternation in his eyes.

"This'll take some time, *M'mselle,*" he said. "The horses are fresh and it'll be hard to keep them standing so long."

"I do not intend to let them stand, Jacques," Yola replied. "I will drive them through the town and look at the country on the other side."

"You'll be all right alone, *M'mselle?*"

"Are you doubting my skill with the reins, Jacques?" Yola asked. "You taught me yourself, and if I cannot drive as well as Papa, it must be your fault!"

The groom laughed.

"You drive well enough, *M'mselle,* for a lady, as you well know."

Yola smiled at the qualification, knowing that she was in fact an extremely expert driver and rider.

"I will come back for you in about twenty minutes, Jacques," she told him. "But do not worry if I am a little longer. It is so exciting to be in the valley again that I might easily forget the time."

Before Jacques could expostulate she had driven away, sitting with a straight back, holding her reins and her whip at the angle which reminded the old groom forcibly of the late *Comte.*

There was a suspicion of tears in his eyes as he watched Yola until she was out of sight, then hurriedly he went into the Pharmacy.

As soon as Yola was out of the town she touched her horses with the whip and they moved swiftly over a narrow road until they reached a small hamlet.

Here she hesitated for a moment before she turned left and a few moments later saw high iron gates opening onto a tree-bordered drive.

She turned her horses up it, the ground rising until ahead she saw a house in grey stone with turrets on either side of it and a double sweep of steps leading to the front door.

It was very small, and yet so attractive that it looked to Yola like a fairy-palace in miniature, and she recognised that it had been built at the same period as her own Castle.

There was a gravel sweep in the front and as she turned her horses in it an aged groom came hurrying from an adjacent stable to go to their heads.

As he did so he noticed the Beauharnais coat-of-arms on the chaise and she saw his eyes look at it with astonishment.

She alighted, and before she reached the front door, as if her arrival had been noticed as she came up the drive, an old servant with white hair stood there bowing respectfully.

"Is *Madame* Renazé at home?" Yola enquired.

"I will enquire, *Mademoiselle,* if she is receiving visitors," the servant replied respectfully.

He went ahead and Yola followed him up a flight of stairs into a small Salon.

One glance told her that it was furnished in exquisite taste, and as the servant bowed and went from the room, closing the door behind him, Yola looked round her.

She knew that the colours, the furnishings, and the very pictures on the walls were exactly what her father liked, and undoubtedly he had chosen them himself.

Then she saw that there was a portrait of him over the mantelpiece.

It must have been painted about fifteen years earlier, and obviously by a very skilled artist, for it was brilliantly done and was a perfect likeness.

There was the twinkle in his eyes that she had always loved, a faint smile on his lips, and he looked both happy and extremely handsome, as if he was listening to something he enjoyed hearing.

'I am here, Papa,' Yola told him wordlessly.

Then she heard the door open and a woman came into the room.

It was easy to recognise her from the miniature which Yola had found in her father's desk, but she was not in fact much older, although she had many grey hairs and there were soft lines at the sides of her sparkling eyes.

It was easy to see that she had lost none of the attractiveness that the artist had portrayed so faithfully, and she walked proudly and with dignity.

There was however an expression of almost incredulous surprise on her face as she advanced towards Yola.

"My servant told me," she said in a low voice, "having recognised the coat-of-arms on your chaise, that *Mademoiselle la Comtesse* had called on me, but I thought he must be mistaken."

"I have come to see you, *Madame*," Yola replied, "because I need your help."

"My help?" *Madame* Renazé repeated. Then she added in a different tone: "Perhaps it is something which concerns your father's estate?"

Yola was well aware that her father in his will had left a considerable sum of money to *Madame* Renazé and the title deeds of the Château in which she lived.

She answered quickly:

"No, *Madame*, it is nothing to do with my father, except that had he been here I could have asked his advice."

"So instead you have come to me?" *Madame* Renazé asked in surprise.

"I feel you are the only person who can help me."

Madame Renazé was still for a moment and it was obvious she could hardly believe what she had heard. Then she said quickly:

"Forgive me, *Mademoiselle*, I am forgetting my manners in my astonishment at meeting you. May I offer you some coffee, or would you prefer wine?"

"A cup of coffee would be very nice," Yola answered.

It was not because she needed it, but because she thought it might disperse the formality of the atmosphere and make it easier for her to say what she intended.

Madame rang a small silver bell that stood on one of the tables and almost immediately the door opened and the old servant stood there.

"Café, s'il vous plaît," she said.

When the door closed behind him she indicated a chair near the window.

"Will you be seated, *Mademoiselle?*" she asked, and occupied the sofa opposite.

Yola sat down, realising that outside the window was a balcony and beyond a fine view of the Valley of the Indre.

As she looked out, *Madame* Renazé inspected her finely drawn profile, then she said:

"I had always heard how beautiful you were, *Mademoiselle,* and the reports were not exaggerated."

"My father was perhaps prejudiced," Yola said with a smile.

"He loved you very deeply."

"And you, *Madame,* made him very happy. I shall always be grateful to you for bringing so much happiness into his life."

She saw *Madame* Renazé's eyes fill with tears, but she would not let them fall and after a moment she said in a voice that was hardly audible:

"I was the most fortunate woman in the world to be privileged to love such a wonderful man."

"Papa felt the same about you," Yola replied. "He told me once that when you came into his life he was almost in despair. He had nothing to look forward to except darkness and depression; then suddenly there was light, and the light was you."

Madame Renazé clasped her hands together, then she said quietly:

"You are very generous, *Mademoiselle,* to say such things to me and to come here, although in fact you ought not to have done so."

"I had every right to do so, knowing how much

you meant to Papa," Yola answered, "and I am glad, so very glad, that you have such a beautiful house and there are so many things in it to remind you of him."

She knew that *Madame* Renazé had always behaved in the most exemplary manner.

She had actually been in Venice with her father when he died, and she had brought the body home, seeing to everything without any fuss or publicity.

When the coffin was handed over at Langeais Station to those she had notified to be ready to receive it, she had disappeared.

She had not come to the funeral, which had been attended, after the *Comte* had lain in state in his own Chapel, by almost everyone in the vicinity, nor had she even sent an identifiable wreath of flowers.

It was only through the gifts to her in the *Comte*'s will that anyone could have guessed how much they meant to each other.

Yola had always known, and because she and her father had talked frankly with each other, the *Comte* had often spoken of *Madame* Renazé.

She could understand that no full-blooded, intelligent man like her father could live with her mother and not find life intolerable.

She wondered now whether, if he had lived, her father would have married *Madame* Renazé.

But he had died before the conventional year of mourning for his wife was over, and it was something that even Yola had not dared to ask him, in case he should think it an intrusion into the secret side of his life.

Now, looking at *Madame* Renazé, Yola thought she was exactly the type of person her father would love.

When she had first known about her she had been a little jealous, but her father had sensed it and had made it clear to her that love was big enough to have many facets and be given to many people.

"In books," he had said, "they always talk about love as if it is a cake which can only be divided into such-and-such a number of slices, and I regret to say that many people are so stupid they think the same way."

He was watching Yola as he spoke to see her reaction to what he was saying.

"Children start when they are quite small," he went on saying. " 'Do you love me more than you love Pierre?' And women always want absolute and complete possession, but that in fact is not natural or possible."

His voice had deepened as he continued:

"Love is boundless, love is something one cannot parcel up into small containers or restrict. I can promise you, my dearest, you will find you can give your love in a hundred different ways and still have a heart which is overflowing with more."

He had gone on to explain to Yola that it was love when one was thrilled by a beautiful view, by a picture, or by a piece of exquisite craftsmanship.

"One gives out something of one's self towards it," he said, "and one receives in return. That is love, as is compassion, pity, the desire to fight injustice, the impulse of mercy."

Yola tried to understand the first time he spoke in such a way and later on he had elaborated what was a fundamental part of his own beliefs.

"I love you, *ma petite*," he said, "with every fibre of my being, with my senses, and with my mind. At the same time, I love other people, but that does not detract from my love for you."

He smiled as he told her:

"In fact, in some ways it is increased. Because one person of whom I am thinking, having made me happy, has made it possible for me to have more happiness to give to others."

Looking at *Madame* Renazé now, Yola realised that there was a softness and gentleness in her expression that she had never known in her mother's.

At the same time, she knew that *Madame* had an intelligence and perhaps a wit which must have delighted her father.

There had been a short silence, as if the two

women were appraising each other. Then *Madame* Renazé said:

"Will you tell me, *Mademoiselle*, how I can help you? You know you have only to ask me for anything that is within my power to give."

"May I say first that I hope you will call me Yola," Yola replied. "The only person who has ever called me that was Papa, but I feel that is how he spoke of me to you."

"He did indeed," *Madame* Renazé replied, "and he was so proud of you and made so many plans for your future."

"Did he ever speak to you of my marriage?" Yola asked.

"He mentioned it several times when we were in Venice."

"What did he say?"

"He said: 'This is a city for lovers, and Yola must come here one day with someone she loves.' He laughed and added: 'Not with me. There are so many places I want to take her, but not here, which is where she should spend her honeymoon, and be as happy as—you and I have—been.'"

Madame Renazé's voice broke for a moment on the last words.

As she groped for the tiny lace handkerchief that was tucked into the belt of her full skirt, the servant came in with the coffee.

When he had left the room and *Madame* was filling the china cups Yola asked:

"Did Papa ever mention the name of anyone he thought I might marry?"

"I think he intended that you should marry a distant cousin, the Marquis de Montereau."

Yola drew in her breath.

"Then it is true what *Grandmère* said."

"But your father also said something you should hear."

"What was that?" Yola asked.

"He said not once but many, many times: 'Yola must never be unhappy as I was made. She must never be forced into a marriage with someone completely incompatible, with different ideas and different ideals. I could not bear her to suffer.' "

Yola gave a sigh that was one of relief.

It was what she felt her father would have intended, and it answered the question she had been asking herself ever since her grandmother had spoken to her.

She bent forward in her chair, her eyes on *Madame* Renazé's face.

"Because Papa said that to you," she said, "because you know how unhappy he himself was with my mother, will you help me?"

"Will you tell me how?" *Madame* Renazé asked simply.

"My grandmother has told me," Yola said, "that she has already written to the Marquis de Montereau to ask him to come and stay at the Castle next month. You know as well as I do that this is equivalent to my being betrothed to him."

"But surely. . . ?" *Madame* Renazé began.

"You do not know my grandmother," Yola interrupted. "Beneath a fragile appearance she has a will of iron. It was she who married Papa, when he was twenty-one, to my mother. She is now determined that I shall marry the Marquis, and I know that once he arrives at the Castle the whole thing will be a *fait accompli.*"

"And you do not wish to marry him?"

"I have never met him, but what I have heard while at school near Paris has made me think that he is unsuitable as a husband."

"Why should you think that?" *Madame* Renazé asked.

"You should understand better than anyone else," Yola replied, "that Papa has brought me up with noble ideals and with the idea that I must have a purpose in my life."

Madame Renazé did not reply and Yola went on:

"From all I have heard of the Marquis, his life is one incessant round of pleasure. I have not lived in

Paris itself, but I have heard of what goes on there, of the extravagant parties, the Balls, and the Masques which take place every night, and of the scandal and gossip which frequently end in duels."

She made a gesture with her hands as she said:

"The Marquis is part of the much-criticised 'Second Empire.' Do you think he would enjoy or tolerate a quiet life at Beauharnais with no audience except for his wife?"

There was silence, then *Madame* Renazé said:

"I have not met the Marquis, but I have heard of him."

"As I have!" Yola added. "And that, *Madame*, is why I want you to help me."

Madame Renazé looked puzzled and Yola explained:

"I want to meet the Marquis but not when he comes to the Castle to meet the girl to whom it belongs. I want to meet him incognito, so I can appraise him as a man, not as a suitor."

Madame Renazé looked startled.

"How could this possibly be achieved?"

"That is what I am asking you," Yola replied.

Now as the two women's eyes met *Madame* Renazé asked incredulously:

"What are you suggesting?"

"May I be very frank without offending you, *Madame*?"

"It would not offend me, whatever you say, my dear," *Madame* replied. "Just believe that I am trying to understand, I am trying to help!"

"What I want to do," Yola answered, "is to meet the Marquis not as a Social *jeune fille*, and certainly not as the chatelaine of Beauharnais, but as someone who belongs to a different world; the world in which, I understand he plays a very important part."

There was silence, then *Madame* Renazé said:

"I understand what you are asking me, but it is impossible! Completely and absolutely impossible!"

"Why?"

"Because you are a lady, because you have been

brought up in a very different way, and you can have no conception of what that which you call the 'other world' is like."

Yola drew in her breath. Then she said:

"And yet you belonged to it, *Madame*, and my father loved you."

Madame Renazé was very still, then she said:

"That was rather different."

"Why?"

"Because I fell in love with your father and because we knew the moment we met that we were meant for each other."

"And so you were brave enough to ignore convention and live with him as his *chère amie* and make him, as he believed himself to be, the happiest man in the world."

Yola smiled as she added:

"I can see nothing wrong in that."

"I am not suggesting it was wrong," *Madame* Renazé said, "but at times it has been difficult, except that I had your father's love and nothing else mattered."

"I too want to fall in love," Yola said, "and I can understand my grandmother's wish that I should marry the Marquis and doubtless as he has no estate of his own that he should own Beauharnais."

She paused before she said positively:

"But I will not be sacrificed on the altar unless I know that the man I marry is someone I love and who loves me for myself."

"Oh, my child, my child, you are asking so much!" *Madame* Renazé cried. "There are thousands and thousands of people in the world who are quite content with their marriage although it is not the wonder and the rapture of a liaison between two people who are meant for each other."

"I think you will understand," Yola said, "that as my father's daughter I will not accept a second-best."

"But . . . this idea of yours . . ."

"I know it sounds outrageous," Yola interrupted, "I knew before I came here that it would doubtless shock you, but it is something I intend to do. I must get to Paris and somehow I must meet the Marquis and see what he is like when he is off his guard."

She paused for a moment before she went on:

"From what I have heard, there is not a party of any importance at which he is not present. Therefore, it should not be hard for me to make his acquaintance."

"Disguised as what?" *Madame* Renazé asked abruptly.

"If I say a *demi-mondaine* you will doubtless be horrified," Yola replied. "Perhaps there is a prettier word for it—I do not know. I could perhaps pretend to be an actress, but I know nothing of the Theatre. But somehow, whether you will help me or not, I intend to meet the Marquis when he has no idea who I am."

She was silent for a moment. Then she said:

"You may think it very conceited, but if I am in any way as Papa described me, perhaps the Marquis would wish to make my acquaintance."

"You are beautiful," *Madame* Renazé answered, "and, as your father always said, in a way unique and different from other women. It should not be difficult for you to attract the Marquis, or any other man you meet. But I just cannot countenance your way of going about it."

"What is the alternative?" Yola asked, speaking in the quiet, logical tone in which she had so often argued with her father. "If he comes here he will hardly see me as a person. He will see the Castle, the estate, the very large fortune I possess, the whole of it in a golden aura."

She threw out her arms.

"You must agree, *Madame*, it would be impossible for a man to decide in his mind what attracted him the most."

"I understand exactly what you are saying to me," *Madame* Renazé answered. "But I cannot envisage how you can do such an unconventional and outrageous thing as going to Paris in disguise and escape being hurt or insulted in the process."

"It will not matter particularly if I am," Yola said. "My business is only with the Marquis, and once I have got to know him, once I have talked to him, I shall know the answer to my question where he is concerned. And actually, I am very quick at making up my mind."

"But what if you dislike him?"

"Then nothing and nobody will make me marry him," Yola answered. "I shall force *Grandmère* to cancel the invitation she has sent him, and even if I have to spend the rest of my life as an old maid I will not have him thrust a wedding-ring on my finger."

"You are right in principle," *Madame* Renazé said, "but it is going to be very hard to put it into practice."

"Then help me," Yola begged. "That is why I have come to you."

Madame Renazé put her hand up to her forehead, then said:

"I have no idea, and if I did I would be afraid to suggest it."

"Shall I tell you when I first thought of coming to you?" Yola asked in a quiet voice. "It was when I was looking at your miniature which I found in father's desk. I had been sitting in his room, talking to him, asking him what I should do."

She paused as she remembered the intensity with which she had asked her father's guidance, and then she went on:

"As there seemed to be no reply from him, I opened the drawers of his desk and found what I am sure are your letters to him and lying on top of them the miniature."

She saw that *Madame* Renazé was listening intently and she went on:

"It was then, just as if Papa were speaking to me, that a plan fell into place in my mind, that I should come to you so that you could arrange for me to go to Paris and enter the 'half-world' which, if what I hear is correct, has encroached upon the Social World, which used to be so select."

"You are right about that," *Madame* Renazé said with a little sigh. "The Emperor has broken down many barriers."

"And also the Marquis de Montereau," Yola added.

"Perhaps—I am not certain about him," *Madame* Renazé said. "But I do know someone who knows him well and who could introduce you without his being in the least suspicious as to your true identity."

Yola's face lit up with a smile.

"Then you will help me, *Madame*?"

"You have rather forced my hand," *Madame* Renazé retorted.

Then suddenly they both laughed.

"This is incredible! Unbelievable!" *Madame* cried. "I always hoped that one day I would meet you, but how could I have imagined in my wildest dreams that you would be sitting here in my house, putting preposterous ideas into my head?"

"*Grandmère* would be so shocked!" Yola laughed. "And so would all my other relations."

"You are not afraid of meeting them in Paris?"

"I have not seen any of them for years," Yola replied. "You know Mama would never have anyone at the Castle, and when she died Papa and I thought it would seem heartless to start entertaining immediately. We decided to wait until the period of mourning was over."

Yola gave a sigh that came from the very depths of her being.

It was in the eleventh month of that mourning that her father had died, and then there had been a further twelve months while she had been at school.

As it happened, she had not been present at her father's funeral, when relatives from all over France had journeyed to Beauharnais to pay their last respects to the head of the family.

Perhaps because she had been so abjectly miserable and so shocked by the suddenness of his dying when he was away from her, she had contracted a form of pneumonia and the Doctor had forbidden her to leave her bed.

She had not minded being absent from her father's funeral. She wanted to remember him not still and lifeless but full of vitality and laughter as he had been the last time she had seen him.

So she had cried alone in her bed-room and an elderly cousin who lived in Tours had played host to all those who must be entertained after the ceremony.

For the first time Yola wondered now if the Marquis had been amongst them.

She had not bothered to enquire who had been present, for she had felt too miserable and ill to care.

Now she wondered if he had appraised the Castle and already made up his mind to be the owner of it.

Aloud she said:

"Tell me the plan you have for me, *Madame*?"

"There is something I wish to explain first," *Madame* Renazé said. "You have spoken of the *demi-mondaines*, and perhaps it is a good word, invented by Dumas *fils*, for the 'half-world' which has gained so much importance in Paris."

She paused before she went on:

"The Second Empire has been called 'the Golden Era of the Courtesans,' but the women who have made Paris the most talked-of city in the world, whose jewels, whose parties, and whose appearance in the Bois have set Europe talking, are very different in every way from someone like myself and my niece."

Yola looked at her enquiringly as she went on:

"Frenchmen since the beginning of time have taken for themselves *chères amies* because they have found that the marriages arranged for them by their parents have often been unhappy or even, like your father's, one of complete misery."

Her eyes were soft as she continued.

"They have fallen in love and in many cases found real contentment with a woman with whom they cannot appear in Society but who to all intents and purposes is a second wife."

"I think I have always understood that," Yola said gently. "And the King's mistresses had an important place at Court and were often more powerful than the Queen."

"That is true," Madame Renazé agreed. "King Louis XIV, after he was widowed, married his mistress *Mademoiselle* de Maintenon, and history tells us that he could not do without her. Many aristocrats have in fact, on becoming widowers, married the women who have supported and helped them during the years of an unhappy marriage."

From the way she spoke, Yola knew that she had hoped one day to marry her father.

Then almost as if she pushed aside the dream-like manner in which she had been speaking, *Madame* Renazé said more briskly:

"My niece, Aimée Aubigny, is the *chère amie* of the *Duc* de Chôlet. The *Duc's* wife is incurably insane and with Aimée he is extremely happy. They hope one day he will be free to marry her."

Yola was listening eagerly as *Madame* went on:

"But of course as far as the real Social World is concerned my niece is not accepted. However, as the *Duc* is an extremely intelligent man, she has gathered round her many writers and men of talent so that her Salon is one of the most important in Paris."

Madame Renazé smiled as she added proudly:

"Second, I am told, only to that of the *Princesse* Matilde."

Yola was aware that this was high praise since the *Princesse* Matilda, cousin of the Emperor and sister of the Prince Napoleon, was noted as being the most intelligent woman in France.

She presided over a Salon which had been called by an accepted writer—"A true Salon of the nineteenth century. No Salon has ever given France so much as the Salon of *la bonne Princesse*."

"I will meet your niece?" Yola asked.

"If you are really intent on what I can only call a daring escapade," *Madame* Renazé replied, "I will write to my niece, explaining what you want and asking if you may stay with her in Paris."

Yola gave a little cry of delight.

"Will you really do that, *Madame*? I shall be so grateful . . . so very grateful."

"I hope you will be able to say that to me again when you return," *Madame* Renazé replied.

"I should feel grateful even if the Marquis turns out to be what I expect."

"Then I will write immediately and I should have a reply within two days," *Madame* Renazé said.

"If your niece will have me, I will leave for Paris immediately I hear from you," Yola said. "Although *Grandmère* has not asked the Marquis to stay until next month, I might not get to know him at once and he might not be interested in me. I must therefore have a little time to play with."

"I still feel I should dissuade you from doing anything so mad," *Madame* Renazé said.

"Nothing you could say or do would prevent me," Yola replied. "You are only making it easier for me and, if you like, safe-guarding me from getting into the wrong part of the *demi-monde*."

Madame Renazé sighed.

"You are so like your father when you want something," she said. "He could always twist me into agreeing with anything he suggested by making it somehow sound quite the right thing, even though I knew it was wrong."

"This is not wrong, this is right!" Yola said positively. "Right for me. And I knew you would not fail me."

She glanced at the clock on the mantelpiece as she spoke, and then rose reluctantly to her feet.

"I must go back," she said. "I have left my groom, Jacques, in the town, and if I am too long he will be in a panic in case I have driven myself into a ditch. The only person he really trusted with his horses was Papa."

"Your father was a magnificent driver," *Madame* Renazé said.

"He was good at everything he did!" Yola smiled. "A good shot, a good employer, and a good father."

She saw the expression in *Madame* Renazé's eyes and knew that she would like to have added: "And a very good lover," but felt it was not the proper thing to say to a young girl.

On an impulse Yola bent and kissed the older woman's cheek.

"You have been so kind, so understanding," she said. "I think Papa would be glad that we are here together."

She looked up at her father's portrait as she spoke.

"You know, *Madame,*" she went on, "nothing would have amused him more than what you call 'this mad escapade.' He would have thought it showed courage and initiative—two things he liked me to have."

"He might also have thought it foolhardy and dangerous," *Madame* Renazé answered.

"How can there be any real danger?" Yola asked. "If things get out of hand I shall just come home."

"I hope it is as easy as that," *Madame* Renazé replied doubtfully.

"I have a feeling that if your niece is like you," Yola said, "she will be warning me and looking after me."

"I hope she will do that," *Madame* Renazé said, "and of one thing I am quite sure, she will find it very amusing. Aimée has a great sense of humour and she will enjoy deceiving the Marquis and perhaps the rest of Paris."

"I am not interested in anybody but him," Yola answered.

As she drove away from the little Château she felt elated and excited in a manner she had not felt since she had returned home.

First there had been the emptiness of the Castle without her father, then the menace that her grandmother had conjured up in speaking of the Marquis.

Now, it was as if the sun had come out and the

shadows had been dispersed, and ahead there was a voyage of discovery that was a real adventure.

'I must plan everything very carefully,' she thought, 'and no-one must be in the least suspicious.'

Flicking her horses with the whip, she hurried them towards Langeais, knowing that Jacques would be waiting and undoubtedly reproachful because she had been so long.

* * *

Yola was having breakfast alone in the small Dining-Room at the Castle when a servant brought her a note on a silver salver.

She took it from him and felt with a sudden leap of her heart that this was what she had been waiting for.

Three days had passed since she had visited *Madame* Renazé and she was beginning to wonder frantically if anything had gone wrong and her niece had refused to entertain such an idea.

Now, in the neat, upright handwriting that she had seen on the letters in her father's desk, was the answer for which she had been waiting.

She did not open the envelope until the servants had left the room.

She breakfasted alone because her grandmother had hers in bed, saying that it was far too chill in the mornings for her to rise until the sun had done so.

The letter from *Madame* Renazé was very brief:

> *My niece, Aimée, will be delighted to welcome you as soon as is convenient to you at her house in the Rue du Faubourg Saint-Honoré. When you reply, will you let her know if you would like a carriage to meet you at the station, or if you will find your own way? I shall be thinking and praying for you, and you know that I wish for your well-being and your happiness.*

The letter was unsigned and Yola knew that *Madame* Renazé was being discreet in case it should fall into the wrong hands.

Yola was well aware that everyone, including the servants in the Castle, would be shocked if they knew she was associating with the woman who had been her father's mistress.

What was more, those who had served the *Comte* for years would think it their duty to tell her grandmother what was occurring, and this might cause endless trouble.

Accordingly, she committed the contents to memory, tore the letter into small pieces and threw them into the fire, then sat down to write to *Madame* Aimée Aubigny.

She did not entrust the letter to anyone in the Castle, but making another excuse to go into the town posted it herself.

Only when it had gone did she return to find her grandmother downstairs in the Salon.

"How are you feeling this morning, *Grandmère?*" Yola asked, kissing her.

"A little warmer, thank you, *ma chérie,*" her grandmother replied, "but you seem to be very thinly garbed for a spring day. Remember, the winds can be treacherous even in the Loire Valley, and you do not want a repetition of your illness of last year."

"It is really quite warm, *Grandmère,*" Yola said, "but actually I do find I want a number of new clothes which I did not have time to buy before I came home."

She did not look at her grandmother as she added:

"If the Marquis is coming here to stay, and I hope . . . other people as well . . . I do not wish to appear like Cinderella in rags and tatters."

"You hardly look like that," her grandmother replied, glancing at the elegant small crinoline that Yola was wearing and the little tight-fitting jacket that matched it.

"I think the Exchequer would run to two or three gowns from Worth, do you not, *Grandmère*?"

She thought her grandmother was hesitating and added:

"I am sure the Marquis, since he is such a 'ladies' man,' has an appreciation of women's clothes."

It was the bait that she knew her grandmother would be unable to resist.

"Yes, of course," the *Comtesse* replied. "You must be properly gowned, and though what you have been wearing seems very attractive I dare say Worth will fit you out as befits your position, and the things you buy can form the basis of your trousseau."

Yola's lips tightened, but she strangled the retort she was about to make before it reached her lips and said quite pleasantly:

"Then the sooner I go to Paris, the better, *Grandmère*. I think I had better leave the day after tomorrow. After all, having ordered what I want, I can return and then go back again if more fittings are needed."

Before her grandmother could speak she gave a little sigh.

"How I hate fittings! Perhaps it would be easier after all to look like Cinderella."

"No, no, of course not!" the *Comtesse* said quickly. "A woman's appearance is always important and it is no use trying to be beautiful in a shabby frame."

"Very well," Yola agreed almost reluctantly, "I will go to Paris, and I shall stay with one of my friends with whom I was at school."

"Would you not like me to write to one of your cousins in the Boulevard Saint-Germain?"

Yola knew that this was the area on the Left Bank in which the majority of the ancien régime had settled, and she thought with a little smile of amusement how horrified they would be if they knew with whom she would really be staying.

"No, thank you, *Grandmère*," she said. "You know as well as I do that they will want to entertain me. They will give afternoon Receptions and family dinner-parties, and I shall never have a chance of getting anything done."

"Perhaps you are right," the *Comtesse* agreed, "but I am sure they would like to see you, if you have time."

"If I have time I promise you I will call on them," Yola said, "but please do not write and tell them I am in Paris. You know they will take umbrage if I cannot accept their invitations."

"I understand," the *Comtesse* conceded.

Even so, Yola thought right up until the last minute that there might be difficulties in getting away, but surprisingly everything seemed to go smoothly.

Her grandmother even accepted that, while one of the elder maids should accompany her to Paris in the train, her friends would rather she did not bring a lady's-maid with her to their house, but would arrange for her to be looked after by their own servants.

Had she been a married woman this would have been inconceivable, but for a young girl it was understandable that she could manage to share a lady's-maid with her friends.

The old maid who acted as chaperon to Yola was only too glad to return to the Castle by the next train.

"I never did like Paris, *M'mselle*," she said disparagingly, "nasty, noisy place, with every likelihood of being run over if one steps off the pavement!"

"I will not be there for long," Yola said. "You must look after my grandmother and see that she has every comfort."

"*Madame* is yearning for the warm sun of the South," the maid replied.

Yola knew this was true, but her grandmother had no intention of being lonely while she was away.

She had already invited a friend as old as herself who lived in Tours to come to the Castle to keep her company and Yola knew they would have plenty to gossip about and would doubtless plan her wedding in detail.

The idea made her all the more eager to reach Paris as quickly as possible.

She had a feeling the sands were running out and unless she was careful she would achieve nothing and the Marquis would arrive full of hope at the Castle. Then the only way she could be rid of him would be to have one devastatingly explosive row both with him and with her grandmother.

This was to be avoided at all costs because she knew the repercussions of it would vibrate through the family.

Her father had been very conscious of his position as head of the Beauharnais family, and although there was nothing he could do about it he had always felt guilty about his wife's inhospitality.

He deeply regretted the manner in which she had alienated himself and his daughter from those of their own blood.

"I must bring them back into the life of the Castle," Yola told herself. "I must not be selfish and want only those who are intellectual and talented round me."

She knew that was how the *Grand Seigneurs* had behaved in the old days, with their relations filling the house so that the great Castles had almost been a city within themselves.

Last night when her grandmother had gone to bed she had walked through the vast rooms feeling how quiet and empty they were.

Then she had gone out onto the terraces on which there were orange trees, some of them having been planted a hundred years earlier.

It was all majestic and impressive, and yet who was there to enjoy it but herself and one old woman who was longing to be somewhere else?

'It is wrong!' Yola thought. 'The Castle should be filled with those both old and young who love it and all it stands for.'

It suddenly occurred to her how wonderful it would be to have children here, not one child, as she had been, lonely, and afraid of the austere, cold woman she called mother, but boys and girls of varying ages.

She walked to the terrace to look out over the sleeping valley.

'I want to have children of my own,' she thought, 'but unless I love a man, how could I bear him to be their father?'

She thought of the Marquis and shivered.

No child of hers must ever think of their father as just a pleasure-seeker, a man who would turn from one woman to another and care for nothing but the gratification of his senses.

She looked up at the sky.

"Send me someone whom I can love, Papa," she prayed. "Send me a man like yourself whose heart is big and whose mind is understanding."

The night was very still. She waited but it seemed to her there was no answer.

Chapter Three

Yola put the maid who had accompanied her to Paris in the Ladies' Waiting-Room and said goodbye to her. She only had an hour to wait before she could catch the train back to Langeais.

Accompanied by a porter carrying her luggage, Yola went outside the station to find waiting for her a very elegant closed carriage with a coachman and a footman on the box.

She noticed with satisfaction that it discreetly had no coat-of-arms or crest emblazoned on it and that the livery of the servants was quiet and not in any way ostentatious.

She had thought during the journey that she was calm and not in the least apprehensive as to what lay ahead. But now as they neared the Rue du Faubourg Saint-Honoré she felt her heart thumping, and she knew that she was in fact feeling nervous about meeting *Madame* Renazé's niece.

The house in the Rue du Faubourg Saint-Honoré stood back a little from the road, and there was a small court-yard by which the carriage entered and drove round a sweep to the front door.

The house was grey and anonymous with wooden shutters, but the moment Yola passed into the Hall she realised that it was in fact furnished in excellent taste and filled with treasures of the type she appreciated.

She could not have lived in the Castle all her

life, surrounded by antique furniture, magnificent pictures, statues, and bronzes, without having learnt a great deal about them.

Her father had been her instructor in teaching her about the various periods of French history when their craftsmen had led the world in almost every branch of art.

Yola had a quick glance at a very fine Louis XV inlaid commode and some Boulle pieces of an even earlier date, then she was shown into a Salon on the ground floor with windows opening onto a garden behind the house.

There, she had no time to notice anything but the woman who rose from a *secrétaire* to cross the room towards her.

Yola had naturally expected that *Madame* Aimée Aubigny would look like her aunt, but there was in fact very little resemblance.

Madame Renazé was beautiful even in her middle age, but her niece could make no claims to real beauty. At the same time, she had an arresting, fascinating face which made one want to look at her and look again.

She had dark eyes that slanted a little at the corners and a mouth which curved in a smile that was infectious. As she held out her hand to Yola there was no doubt that the welcome which she expressed with her lips was sincere.

"I am delighted to meet you, *Mademoiselle la Comtesse*," she said, "and may I say I am very honoured that you will stay here as my guest."

"I have so much to thank you for," Yola replied, "and I only hope you will not regret befriending me."

"I will not do that," Aimée Aubigny said, "and quite frankly, it is the most adventurous thing I have heard of anyone undertaking."

Her eyes seemed to be laughing and Yola found herself laughing too.

"Your aunt has already told me it is outrageous," she replied, "but you do understand that it is something I have to do?"

"I understand, and I commend you for your courage," Aimée Aubigny said.

She made a gesture with her hand as she added:

"Please sit down. Now we must plan everything very quickly, because no-one in this household must have any idea who you really are."

"You mean the servants?" Yola questioned. "Certainly everything must be kept hidden from them."

"It must indeed," Aimée Aubigny agreed. "In Paris everyone talks. The chatter of the servants is unceasing and everything that is said or done sweeps along the grapevine to the other houses, so that it is almost impossible to keep a secret."

"I must keep mine," Yola said.

She thought as she spoke how horrified her grandmother and her other relations would be if they had the least idea of what she was doing at this moment.

"First of all," *Madame* Aubigny said, "we must choose a name for you, if you have not done so already."

"No, I was going to consult you about that," Yola replied. "I thought I would call myself 'Yola' because no-one has ever used that name for me except my father. To everyone else I am Marie Teresa."

" 'Yola' is charming!" Aimée Aubigny said. "And, as you are so beautiful, why not 'Yola Lefleur.' That will suit you. It sounds a little theatrical, which after all is what we want."

"I am delighted with your suggestion," Yola answered.

"Then that is settled. In this household you will be an old friend whom I have not seen for some years, and whom I am introducing to Paris. That in fact is the story we will tell everyone."

She looked at Yola a little critically, so that she asked:

"Are you thinking I must change my appearance?"

"Only your clothes," Aimée Aubigny answered.

"My clothes?" Yola questioned.

"They are very suitable for a *jeune fille* but would look out of place, I think, if you intend to appear a little older, which is essential."

"How old?" Yola enquired.

Again *Madame* Aubigny examined her critically.

"I think," she said after a moment, "with your hair done in a different manner and with the right gowns, you will be able to pass for twenty-two or twenty-three."

Yola had not thought this was necessary, and as she looked enquiringly at her hostess, Aimée Aubigny explained:

"No-one would expect me to chaperon a young girl or to introduce someone who has only just left the School-Room into my way of life."

"No, I understand," Yola said.

"You will therefore have to be a close friend. I make no pretence about being twenty-seven. You must be old enough to understand the world in which you are ready to play a part."

Yola looked a little startled, then said in a low voice:

"Of course, I understand."

"That is why it is important," Aimée Aubigny said, "that we should go at once to buy the right kind of gowns for *Mademoiselle* Lefleur."

"I am ready now," Yola said with a smile.

"You would not like to rest first and have something to eat and drink?"

"No, thank you. I had luncheon on the train," Yola replied, "and because the Chef at Beauharnais felt that to go to Paris was as adventurous as making my way to Tibet or up to the top of Mont Blanc, he provided far more than I could possibly eat."

"Very well then," Aimée Aubigny said. "I told them to keep the carriage, and the sooner we leave the less likely it is that anyone will see you as you are now."

Yola could not help feeling that this was a little disparaging to the very elegant travelling-costume she wore, which she had purchased for her return to the Castle.

However, she knew she must leave everything to Aimée Aubigny's good sense, and when they were ready to leave the house she saw all too clearly the difference in their appearance.

Madame Aubigny was in fact dressed very simply in black, but it was black as only a Parisian *Couturier* could make it.

There were touches of white and an elegant trimming of braid, and it was cut so as to reveal her slim and yet beautifully curved figure.

Yola did not miss the fact that the jewels she wore were few but quite superb.

As they got into the carriage Aimée Aubigny said:

"You will understand of course that I must call you by your Christian name and you will not think it too familiar."

"I will say the same to you," Yola replied with a smile.

"Very well, Yola," Aimée replied. "I think this is going to be a very exciting adventure, but we must be careful, very careful, that no-one, not even my dearly beloved *Duc*, has any idea that you are not who you pretend to be."

"Only your aunt knows my secret," Yola said, "and she has been exceedingly kind to me."

"She is a wonderful person," Aimée replied, "and she was so happy with your father after being so utterly and completely miserable when she was your age."

"I know nothing about her past," Yola said, "except, I suppose, that she was married to a *Monsieur* Renazé."

"She was indeed. She was married when she was seventeen and it was a nightmare of misery and unhappiness until finally her husband died."

Yola made a little murmur of sympathy and Aimée went on:

"I suppose you do not know that Aunt Gabrielle's father, my grandfather, was a very clever man."

"Tell me about him," Yola begged.

"He was a scholar and wrote a number of books, mostly rather dull and appreciated only by scholars like himself, but he was respected and admired in Bordeaux, where he lived."

She paused as if she was looking back into the past before she went on:

"Unfortunately, he found his family rather a bore, and when he had a chance of marrying off his daughters he did not hesitate."

"Marriage is something which always seems to occupy the thoughts of our relations," Yola said a little bitterly.

"My grandfather and grandmother were no exception," Aimée said, "and Aunt Gabrielle, who was very beautiful, was married to a man of fifty, who was, however, a gentleman of some importance in the vicinity of Bordeaux."

"And she obviously had no choice in the matter."

"Of course not," Aimée agreed. "She was frightened of him and she actively disliked him from the moment they were married. But none of that counted beside the fact that Aunt Gabrielle's father and mother were impressed by their new son-in-law."

"You say she was unhappy?" Yola asked.

"*Monsieur* Renazé drank and had a habit of taking out his temper on his horses and his wife," Aimée said. "It was the most fortunate thing that could have happened when one of his horses, unable to stand such treatment, threw him at a high jump and caused him to break his neck."

"And so your aunt was free."

"Only for a very short while," Aimée answered with a smile. "She came to Paris, met your father, and they fell in love."

"So her story had a happy ending after all."

"Just as I hope yours will," Aimée replied. "I understand and sympathise with everything you are doing, and because I knew what had happened to Aunt Gabrielle I was determined that I would never suffer as she did."

She paused before she added:

"When my parents told me they had arranged my marriage for me, I ran away."

"Where did you go?" Yola asked.

"I came to Paris," Aimée answered, "and fortunately I knew one or two people who moved in what were called 'smart circles.'"

She went on to tell Yola how first she had been taken under the protection of a young aristocrat with whom she fancied herself to be very much in love.

"I was soon disillusioned," Aimée said, "and it was entirely my own fault that I was deceived by his good looks, his charm, and the innocent belief that I was the only woman in his life."

"When you found out the truth were you very unhappy?" Yola enquired.

"Desperately, but only for a short while," Aimée said lightly. "Paris is very gay and very alluring and it was easy to forget. There were so many other men paying court to me."

Yola waited, and after a moment Aimée went on:

"I had learnt my lesson the hard way and I was determined not to be deceived a second time. I refused a number of invitations, some of them very glamorous, and then I met the *Duc*."

"Did you know at once that you were in love with him?" Yola enquired.

"Almost at once," Aimée answered, "but I was determined not to make a fool of myself, and therefore I was very cautious and played for time."

"What happened?" Yola asked interested.

"Eventually I realised what a wonderful person he was," Aimée answered, "and how much he had to give me."

She saw the expression in Yola's face and added hastily:

"I do not mean money. I am talking of things

that are not material. I always tell him now that he has taught me everything I know of beauty and art, and I think too he has given me an understanding of people."

"*Madame* Renazé said that you had a Salon that was equal to *Princesse* Matilde's."

"Aunt Gabrielle is flattering me," Aimée said. "It is entirely due to the *Duc* that we entertain men of letters and creative ability. I am, from the world's point of view, only the mistress of a very famous man."

Her voice softened as she went on:

"But those who come to my house, or whom we entertain at the *Duc*'s, never make him aware of it, and they treat me in the same way that they would treat the Empress. That is very important from my point of view."

"Of course it is," Yola agreed.

Then because he was never far from her thoughts, she said in a low voice:

"Your aunt said that you know the Marquis de Montereau."

"I know him well," Aimée replied, "but because I think it is important for you to make up your own mind about him, because I think that second-hand impressions are always odious, I am not going to tell you about him. But you will meet him tomorrow evening."

She saw the expression in Yola's eyes and laughed.

"I know you are longing to ask me a thousand questions," she said, "but believe me, I am being wise when I tell you that you will answer them yourself after you have met Leo, as everyone in Paris calls him."

As she spoke, the carriage drew up outside a shop in the Rue de la Paix and Yola glanced out the window, expecting that they would be outside number 6.

This was where Charles Frederick Worth created gowns which always introduced the latest fashion and which were slavishly accepted by almost every woman in Paris from the Empress downwards.

To her surprise, however, she found that they were at the other end of the street, and as the footman got down to open the carriage door Aimée explained:

"We have been talking so much that I have not had time to tell you why we are not visiting Worth. For one thing, he is a gossip, and by tomorrow all Paris would know that he had transformed you into something different from your appearance on arrival in his Salon."

"I did not think of that," Yola exclaimed.

"Also, I think that Pierre Floret," Aimée went on, "who is a genius in his own way, is the right designer for this particular occasion."

"Again, I can only say thank you," Yola replied with a smile.

They stepped out of the carriage and walked into the shop.

The Salon was on the first floor and when Aimée arrived she was greeted with an impressive welcome by the *Vendeuse*, who asked them to be seated while she sent for *Monsieur* Floret.

"Pierre Floret is a young man," Aimée explained. "He is ambitious and has an artistic genius such as Worth had when he first came to Paris."

"I thought *Monsieur* Worth was still," Yola said.

"He is," Aimée agreed, "but he has become very blasé."

She smiled and added:

"Who shall blame him? Because the Empress will order from no-one else, he has every other woman in Paris on her knees begging him for something original, something different, so that she will stand out among the thousand other women asking for the same thing."

Yola laughed.

"Pierre Floret is only twenty-two," Aimée continued, "but you will see that his mind and his talent are a hundred years in advance of his age."

As Pierre Floret bowed politely over Aimée's

hand and apologised for having kept her waiting, Yola thought that he looked both intelligent and artistic. He was a very thin young man who looked as if he seldom had time to eat.

When Aimée explained to him that Yola required gowns to make her look older and very sophisticated he asked no questions.

He merely looked at her with the appraising eye of an artist and she felt that he took in not only every detail of her appearance but also her character and personality, so that he could reflect them in what she was to wear.

"This is very important, *Monsieur* Floret," Aimée said. "Very important indeed, both to me and to my dear friend."

Pierre Floret seemed to pause for a moment as if he was considering something. Then he said:

"You have been very kind to me, *Madame*, and I owe at least half my business to your patronage. Now I will repay a little of what I owe you."

"How will you do that?" Aimée enquired.

He lowered his voice so that they could not be overheard and said:

"I am sure I do not have to tell you that every *Couturier* keeps his latest collection under lock and key until the moment he shows it to the public."

"Yes, and I have heard that a great deal of spying goes on between you all," Aimée said with a smile.

"We are working now on our autumn collections," *Monsieur* Floret continued. "The *petite* crinoline, the creation of *Monsieur* Worth, has swept Paris; now everyone is waiting to know what will appear in August."

"I too am waiting," Aimée said. "Are we to dispense with the hoop altogether?"

"My secret, which I will tell only to you," Pierre Floret said, "is that I already know what the great *Monsieur* Worth has in mind."

Aimée's eyes sparkled.

There was nothing a Frenchwoman loved more

than to know what was to be the *dernier cri* before anybody else.

"Tell me—tell me what it is!" she begged excitedly.

"I will not only *tell* you," *Monsieur* Floret replied. "I will *show* you, if you and your friend will come with me."

"But of course," Aimée said, rising to her feet.

She and Yola followed Pierre Floret from the Salon into the back of the building where there were small fitting-rooms.

Beyond them at the end of a passage was a door. He drew a key from his pocket and unlocked it.

"I keep my sewing-room secret from all the rest," he said, "and this is where I hide the finished productions."

He opened the door of what proved to be a small room.

There were a few gowns, only about a dozen and a half, hanging from a steel bar.

He took down one and held it up. Both Aimée and Yola gasped.

It was a gown not only without a crinoline—but everything had been swept from the sides to the back.

It was obvious the gown would mould the figure from the front with an almost Grecian-like closeness, then fall from the waist into a long train.

It was so elegant, so lissom, and so graceful that Yola wondered why anyone had ever thought the crinoline was anything but stiff and unnatural!

"So this is the latest vogue!" Aimée said almost reverently.

Monsieur Floret picked another gown and yet another from where they were hanging.

The décolletage was low and still off the shoulders, the waist very small, and the arms displayed except for a few ruffles of lace or a cluster of ribbons.

The skirts with their fullness at the back were sometimes caught up at the sides with garlands of flowers. Others fell in a cascade of frills and lace in a train.

"This is what my friend, *Mademoiselle* Lefleur, must wear tomorrow night!" Aimée cried.

Monsieur Floret looked astonished.

"Tomorrow night, *Madame*?"

"Why not?" Aimée enquired. "The *Duc* is giving a party at his house in the Champs Élysées. There is to be a large dinner and afterwards many more people will join us. I wish *Mademoiselle* Lefleur to be sensational, and could she be anything else in a gown like that?"

Monsieur Floret thought for a moment, then he said:

"*Madame*, you are right. I intended to keep these as a surprise for a party to be given for the Prince of Wales, who is arriving anyday now to see the Exhibition, or else for the one at the Tuileries when the Czar Alexander comes to Paris with his two sons."

Aimée smiled.

"You know as well as I do that the crush in the Tuileries will be so tremendous that no-one will be able to see anything."

"That is true," *Monsieur* Floret murmured.

"What is more," Aimée went on, "if the Empress is outshone in her own Palace she will be furious, and there might be repercussions which would hurt you."

"You are right, *Madame*, you are always right!" Pierre Floret exclaimed. "Let your friend *Mademoiselle* Lefleur introduce the new fashion to Paris ahead of *Monsieur* Worth. He will be furious but there will be nothing he can do, because I understand that a large number of gowns in his collection have already been completed."

Once the decision was made, Yola had only to be fitted into one of *Monsieur* Floret's beautiful creations and it had to be altered slightly. Then, having ordered dozens more to be made at breakneck speed, they drove back towards the Rue du Faubourg Saint-Honoré.

"I shall feel very shy of appearing different from anyone else," Yola said.

"It is the dream of every woman to be different," Aimée replied, "but remember, we have a great deal more to do. I told the servants before we left the house that Felix is to be there when we return."

"Who is Felix?"

"The supreme hairdresser in all Paris," Aimée answered, "and there is nothing he will enjoy more than creating a new coiffure specially for you. He always tells me how bored he is with the same faces that he sees day after day."

There was no doubt, Yola thought, that Felix was an artist.

He considered her for a long time, looking at her from every angle, walking round and round her like a hungry panther, which he rather resembled.

Then he swept her long black hair back from her forehead and arranged it with the skill and expertise of a great creator.

"No curls," he muttered, "definitely no curls! *Mon Dieu!* But how bored I am with curls."

"Women think it makes them look young," Aimée said, smiling as she sat in Yola's bed-room and watched the *coiffeur* at work.

"Hair will not alter the face, *Madame*, only frame it," Felix replied.

"That is true; and while my friend's hair is very lovely only now has it been shown to its best advantage."

"I have created something new for her," Felix replied, speaking, Yola thought, as if she were not there. "Tomorrow when I do it again I will arrange her jewels in it."

Yola said nothing, but she knew it was because she was in Aimée's company that the hairdresser assumed she would wear a large number of jewels.

When Felix finished, Aimée clapped her hands.

"You look lovely!" she said. "But older—definitely older. And now Jeanne will make up your face."

Every woman in Paris used cosmetics, but Yola, being a *jeune fille*, had used only a very little powder with just a touch of faint pink lip-salve when she left school.

Now Aimée's lady's-maid took her hand, exclaiming as she did so:

"*M'mselle* has the skin of a magnolia!"

"That is what I thought," Aimée said.

When she had finished, Yola looked at her reflection with surprise.

She had no idea that just a touch of mascara on her eye-lashes, the faintest bloom of rouge on her cheeks, and a skilfully applied salve on her lips could make such a difference.

She realised that because she was moving in the circle of the *demi-mondaines*, however exclusive Aimée was, she must expect to be made up far more than anyone in the Social World.

Even so, her lips were not as red as Aimée's, for Yola's whole mouth constituted the only patch of colour about her. She was sure her pale cheeks and skilfully mascaraed lashes were her way of looking different.

Since tonight they were to dine with no-one but the *Duc*, Aimée lent Yola one of her own gowns.

"He must see you as everyone else will," she said, "and I want it fixed in his mind that you are a young woman who can take care of herself and has come to Paris merely to look for amusement."

Accordingly, she lent Yola a small crinoline of black lace over pale pink satin.

It was a simple yet provocative gown, and when she was ready Yola went to Aimée's bed-room to see if she approved.

"Very attractive!" her hostess said. "But it is nothing compared to the way you will look tomorrow night! I think it needs some jewels—otherwise you look too unsophisticated."

"I have nothing very spectacular with me," Yola replied. "There are some very fine jewels in the Beauharnais collection, but they are in the Bank and I was afraid my grandmother might become suspicious if I had wanted to take them with me to Paris."

"What is more, the Marquis might recognise them!" Aimée added. "You must be very careful and never let anything connect you with the Beauharnaises."

"Yes, of course, I am aware of that," Yola said.

"For tonight I will lend you a small diamond necklace of my own," Aimée went on. "It is what I always wear with that gown and I think you will admire it."

This was an understatement. The diamond necklace had huge black pearls hanging from it and was a unique and very lovely piece of jewellery.

There was a bracelet of diamonds and black pearls to match, and when Yola went into the Salon where the *Duc* was waiting she thought it would be impossible for him to think of her as a *jeune fille*.

She had expected him to be attractive and she was not mistaken. A man of forty-five, he was not only handsome but had an air of authority which reminded her of her father. He also had the charm and the courtesy of his generation.

"May I welcome you, *Mademoiselle* Lefleur, to Paris?" he asked. "Aimée tells me you have not been here before."

Yola sank in a deep curtsey and when she rose she answered:

"No, Your Grace, and it is very kind indeed of Aimée to have me to stay. I have been so looking forward to this visit."

"We must do our best to amuse you and to see that your impression of Paris is a favourable one," the *Duc* said.

While he spoke politely, he found it difficult, Yola realised, not to look only at Aimée.

There was no doubt that he was as deeply in love with her as she was with him, and when they talked at dinner Yola thought it would be difficult to find two more fascinating and interesting people.

The *Duc* had a wit which made them laugh, and he had a way of making everything he talked about so interesting that Yola could understand why Aimée listened entranced.

But she also contributed to the conversation and had a gaiety and *joie de vivre* which made her sparkle like the jewels she wore round her neck and wrists.

She was so fascinating that Yola found herself watching her with wide eyes, finding it almost impossible to think of anything to say herself.

She could understand how easy it had been for anyone so attractive to be a success when she came to Paris and that she had a wide choice of men who were all too anxious to constitute themselves her protector.

She had certainly chosen wisely and well, Yola thought, and she found herself hoping fervently that the *Duc's* wife would die so that these two people who were so admirably suited to each other would get married.

"Yola is greatly looking forward to your party tomorrow night," Aimée told the *Duc* before he left them to return to his own house.

"It is your party, as you well know," he answered, and every word he spoke was a caress.

Aimée smiled at him.

"I often wonder how many people would accept my invitations if they were not certain you would be there," she answered.

"Far more than would accept mine without you," he replied, and they both laughed.

When the *Duc* had gone, Yola said:

"I would not like you to think me inquisitive, Aimée, but if I had not been here, would not the *Duc* have stayed with you?"

Aimée smiled.

"We spend a great deal of time together," she said, "but in public the *Duc* is always insistent that I should not appear unconventional. In fact, however, people are well aware of the relationship between us."

She saw the puzzled expression on Yola's face and explained:

"The *Duc* is a great gentleman. He wishes to protect my reputation and to make it as easy as possible for him to look after me, without my sinking to the level of women whose behaviour is a by-word for everything that is vulgar and licentious."

"I understand," Yola said. "Forgive me for being curious."

"Often we go away together," Aimée continued, "for a week or perhaps for only a few days, to the *Duc*'s Château outside Paris, which belongs to him personally and is not part of the Chôlet estates."

She gave a little sigh before she added:

"Then we behave as if we were married as we want to be. But here in Paris he keeps up his position as *Duc*, and I keep up mine as the witty, amusing *Madame* Aubigny whose Salon is sought after and enjoyed."

She paused before adding wistfully:

"But which is not patronised by the ladies of the *Haute Société* who attend the Balls at the Tuileries."

Impulsively Yola bent forward and kissed Aimée's cheek.

"One day," she said, "when you are the *Duchesse* de Chôlet, everyone will come to your parties. In fact they will tear out their hair and bite their nails if they do not receive an invitation!"

"That is what I hope will happen," Aimée answered. "In the meantime, make no mistake, I am very happy, and no-one could be more wonderful to me than the *Duc*."

The following day there was so much to do that Yola had little time to think about the party that lay ahead.

There were not only fittings with *Monsieur* Floret but there was a visit to the milliner, to the glove-maker, and to the shoe-maker.

Practically everything she possessed was either not up-to-date enough or not the right colour to match her new gowns.

She purchased some entrancing small sun-shades to protect her from the sun and Aimée promised that the following day they would go driving in the Bois after having made a sensational first appearance.

"You are making me feel quite nervous about it all," Yola protested. "Supposing I am a flop and nobody notices me?"

"They will notice you!" Aimée prophesied. "I have persuaded the *Duc* to enlarge the party a little. We shall now be fifty for dinner, and among them are several ladies who fancy they lead the fashion and who, I am quite certain, will die with envy when they see you."

"I hope not!" Yola laughed.

"You do not know how much it matters to a Frenchwoman to be more *chic* than anyone else," Aimée said. "The gowns they buy and discard if thrown into the Seine would block it from one bridge to the next!"

"I was astonished at the price when I bought some gowns before I went home," Yola said.

"It gets worse every year, every season," Aimée agreed, "but then money has ceased to have any meaning, owing of course to women like La Païva and Hortense Schneider."

Yola knew that Hortense Schneider was an actress who had sprung into fame and was now the talk of Paris in *The Grand Duchess of Gerolstein.*

As if Aimée realised she was interested, she explained:

"Her dressing-room at the Théâtre de Variétés has become one of the gathering places of Royalty and dignitaries from other countries who are visiting the Exhibition. I am told that the King of Greece and Leopold of Belgium are there almost every night, watching her."

"Is she a good actress?" Yola asked.

Aimée shrugged her shoulders.

"She is certainly a successful one, and perhaps even more successful in her second—or should I say her first?—profession, that of a Courtesan. I am told that the Prince of Wales had already written to say that he requires tickets for her performance—and I will tell you a rather amusing joke about her."

"What is that?"

"The day before yesterday," Aimée said, "*Mademoiselle* Schneider decided to visit the Exposition in the Champs de Mais, and when her carriage arrived she attempted to enter through the Porte d'Iena, which is reserved for visiting Royalty."

"What happened?" Yola asked.

"When the guards insisted on barring her way, she cried out imperiously:

" 'Make way! I am the Grand Duchess of Gerolstein!' "

Aimée laughed as she went on:

"In real Parisian style, the guards took off their hats, bowed low, and let her pass. It certainly shows how important she is."

"It does indeed," Yola agreed. "I would like to see her on the stage."

"We must go one evening," Aimée said, "or perhaps someone else will be taking you."

Yola said nothing, but she could not help feeling how incredible it was that she might go to a Theatre alone with a man.

She could imagine what her grandmother would say if she heard of it.

She knew quite well that Aimée was suggesting that if she was a success with the Marquis, as she hoped she would be, he would show her the sights of Paris and those would doubtless include Hortense Schneider.

Yola had expected to go with Aimée to the *Duc*'s house in the Champs Élysées, but she was told that that would be a mistake.

"I shall be there before the guests arrive," Aimée said, "and I want you not to be seen with me but to appear after everyone else has arrived!"

Yola looked surprised and Aimée said:

"It is all a question of timing, and for you to be the sensation I expect you to be, it is important that you should make your entrance alone."

"You sound as if you are producing me on a stage."

"That is exactly what I am doing," Aimée replied. "This is your big moment, the moment when every eye will be on you. I am only sorry I cannot have a roll of drums to herald your entrance."

"I am feeling nervous enough as it is," Yola said, laughing.

"Remember, the only person who really matters is the Marquis," Aimée said. "He undoubtedly will notice you but I assure you that every other woman in the room will be doing her best to keep him interested in her alone."

"Is he really so attractive?" Yola asked, and there was a cynical note to her voice.

"Wait and see," Aimée replied enigmatically.

Before she left for the *Duc's* house, Aimée went to her guest's bed-room.

Yola certainly looked very different from the girl who had arrived in Paris the previous day. Even to herself Yola had to admit that she looked both interesting and beautiful.

She turned round from the mirror as Aimée entered to stand looking at her across the bed-room. Then her hostess clapped her hands.

"*C'est ravissante* that gown!" she exclaimed. "And you, my dear, are a new star in the firmament over whom all Paris will go mad!"

"I am not at all sure that I shall even appear," Yola said. "I have 'first-night nerves' and my heart is beating alarmingly!"

"That is excellent!" Aimée replied. "Only a very insensitive and mundane woman could do what you are doing tonight and remain unmoved."

"I only hope I do not fail you after all the trouble you have taken."

"You will not do that," Aimée replied. "And now I have brought you the jewels I want you to wear."

Yola raised her eye-brows.

"I thought you told Felix I was not to wear any."

"I wanted Felix to decorate your hair with just three red roses," Aimée replied, "and I must say he has done it very successfully."

Yola's coiffure was in fact a masterpiece.

It revealed her high, intelligent-looking forehead, then swept her dark hair to the back of her head in thick plaits that were almost like a halo above a large chignon.

The hairdresser had fixed just at the right angle three perfect roses which were coming into bloom.

Blood red, they echoed the colour of her silk gown, which seemed to flow from her waist like a river.

The lace, which was dyed to match, showed provocative glimpses of her white skin at the décolletage and where it encircled the tops of her arms.

The gown was sensational because it revealed every line of Yola's perfect body in the front.

There was something Grecian about it, and yet the fullness at the back was almost as if the crinoline had been blown away to appear like waves following the figure-head of a ship.

Never before had Yola realised how white and velvety her skin was and that her eyes could be so large and mysterious above her red lips.

Aimée opened the box she carried in her hand and Yola saw that it contained a necklace of large, perfect rubies, each glowing like the heart of a fire.

"This is what you need," she said.

"They are magnificent!" Yola exclaimed. "But will people not think it strange that I own anything so valuable?"

"They will wonder who gave them to you, and that will keep them speculating for this evening, at any rate," Aimée replied.

She herself had chosen her inevitable black, but with it she wore long emerald ear-rings that matched her necklace.

Yola looked at her, then she said:

"You are so attractive, Aimée, that I have an uncomfortable feeling that while you are there nobody will look at me."

"They will look at you tonight," Aimée promised, "and I assure you I will only allow the *Duc* to talk to you for a few minutes. Then I shall keep him fully occupied."

"You are quite safe," Yola answered. "When you are there, I find, as he does, that it is impossible to look at anything or anybody else."

"You flatter me," Aimée replied, smiling. "My dear, I wish you everything you wish yourself. I only hope that tomorrow you will tell me that our masquerade has been successful."

"And that is what it is," Yola said to herself as she drove alone to the *Duc's* house in the Champs Élysées, leaving the Rue du Faubourg Saint-Honoré a few minutes after Aimée, as she had been told to do.

She was very impressed by the porticoed entrance to the *Duc's* mansion, the flunkeys in resplendent green and gold livery, and the lofty Hall.

The Salon was filled with treasures but she barely noticed them as she passed through to the Winter Garden, where she had learnt they were to assemble before dinner.

"There is a flight of steps down into it," Aimée had told her. "Stand at the top of them for a moment, looking round as if you were searching for me, then descend them very slowly, letting people see both you and your gown."

Now that the moment was upon her, Yola felt shy.

She had a sudden longing to run away; to go back to the Castle and meet the Marquis at the beginning of the next month, as her grandmother wished her to do.

"Why should I go to all this trouble for him?" she asked herself.

Then she knew it was entirely on her own account that she had come to Paris and was pretending to be a very different person from her real self.

'I have to know the truth about him,' she thought. 'I have to see him as he is, not as he will pretend to be when he is trying to marry the Castle and the Beauharnais estates.'

She heard the sound of voices and laughter; then, having paused for a moment in front of a gilt-framed mirror to see that everything was in place, she took off one of her gloves and put her hand up to the ruby necklace as if it would give her strength.

'Rubies are supposed to be lucky,' she told herself, 'especially for those whose birth-stone they are.'

She had been born in July and the ruby was therefore her own birth-stone, and she thought that perhaps it was a lucky omen that Aimée had chosen them without knowing that they had a special meaning for her.

The Major-Domo was waiting to announce her but she still lingered, touching the faint colour on her cheeks and noticing the crimson of her lips, which echoed the colour of the rubies.

She only hoped that her eyes had a touch of fire in them and that they did not show the sudden fear which seemed to grip her within her breast.

Her fingers were very cold when they touched her skin.

Then she slipped her glove on again and, moving forward, showed the Major-Domo without words that she was ready.

He passed through a draped curtain and she followed him.

"*Mademoiselle* Lefleur, Your Grace!" he announced, and Yola moved forward, feeling for a moment as if she were rooted to the ground.

She had a quick impression of plants and flowers, of cages filled with exotic birds, and of a congregation of people who were chattering as if they too were in a cage.

She looked round and realised that her eyes

could not focus, so she could not pick out Aimée from the other women present.

Then slowly, conscious of her train moving slowly behind her, she descended the stairs.

As she reached the bottom she realised that the *Duc* was in front of her, holding out his hand, and she clung to it as if it were a life-line to prevent her from drowning.

"Welcome, *Mademoiselle* Lefleur," he said. "I am so delighted to see you here."

He drew her forward, then Aimée was beside her, kissing her lightly on her cheek.

"You did that perfectly!" she whispered so that no-one else could hear.

Yola forced a smile to her lips.

"There are so many people to whom I wish to introduce you," Aimée continued, "but first you must meet my dear friend the *Comtesse* de . . ."

Yola did not hear the name any more than she heard the names of the next dozen or so women to whom she was introduced.

Then Aimée said:

"Now I want to present you to His Imperial Highness Prince Napoleon!"

As if she had been given her cue by an experienced Stage-Manager, Yola swept down in a low curtsey to the man who stood in front of her.

As she did so she remembered all she had heard about him, and she was disappointed in his appearance.

When she had listened to her father reading his speeches, she had imagined him to be tall and good-looking. Instead, he was comparatively short; yet, he had a distinctive face, even though there was certainly nothing handsome about it.

"How could you have found anything so unique?" Prince Napoleon asked the *Duc*. "A light who has not shone in Paris before!"

"*Mademoiselle* Lefleur is a friend of Aimée's," the *Duc* replied.

"Then it is you whom I should scold, *Madame*,"

the Prince said, "or shall I instead thank you from the bottom of my heart for introducing me to someone so attractive?"

"You are making me shy," Yola said, feeling that something was expected of her.

"Then later I shall do my best to make you feel even more shy," the Prince promised.

There was an expression in his eyes which Yola knew was a danger signal.

Aimée next introduced her to a famous playwright. Then, so suddenly that it came as a shock, Yola heard her say:

"And now you must meet a very old friend—the Marquis de Montereau!"

For a moment Yola felt as if the man's face in front of her swam so that it was impossible to distinguish his expression or anything else about him.

Then she saw two dark eyes looking down into hers and realised that he was in fact different from what she had expected.

While Aimée was explaining how Yola had just come to Paris and that they had been friends for many years, Yola was thinking that the Marquis had the strangest, most unusual face of any man she had ever seen before.

It was not only that he was handsome and taller than she had anticipated; it was that his expression was so arresting.

His eyes twinkled and there was a smile on his lips as if life was a tremendous joke and it was impossible to take anything very seriously.

There was also a twist to his lips, which gave him a mocking look, and Yola had the idea that he was well aware that she had made a deliberately sensational entrance and was amused by it.

"My friend can stay with me for only a short time," Aimée was saying, "and the *Duc* and I have promised to show her everything that is amusing in Paris and make her realise how much she misses by living in the country."

"I hope I may assist in this formidable task," the Marquis answered.

Aimée laughed.

"We have not included you in our calculations, Leo, because we know how full your engagement-book is."

"Engagements were made to be cancelled."

"Then I hope we may rely on you," Aimée said, "but that is not your reputation."

"You are slandering me," the Marquis protested, "and giving *Mademoiselle* Lefleur an entirely false impression!"

He looked at Yola and said:

"Please do not listen to your friend. I assure you I am very reliable, and if I say I will do a thing, I will! And I intend, if you will allow me, to show you Paris."

"I would not listen to him," Aimée said. "Tomorrow morning he will remember a thousand different reasons why he cannot keep the promises he made this evening."

"In which case," Yola said, "I will try not to get excited at the anticipation of something which may never take place."

"You are being extremely unkind to me tonight," the Marquis complained to Aimée. "What have I done to find myself in your black book?"

"You are never in that, Leo," she replied. "I am only concerned that Yola should be as amused and happy as I wish her to be."

"Then you can depend on me," the Marquis said.

"I wonder!" Aimée answered enigmatically.

Then she deliberately drew Yola away to introduce her to other guests.

Yola found herself hoping that the Marquis would wish to talk to her again; but she should have trusted Aimée, for she found herself sitting next to him at dinner.

"I hope you will not take seriously the vile aspersions cast upon me by our mutual friend," he said.

"I have always known Aimée to be very truthful," Yola answered.

"Where you are concerned it would be impossible to be anything else," he replied.

They fenced with each other and Yola found herself amused by the adroit way in which he would turn a phrase to his advantage and say things that made her laugh almost despite herself.

She was finding it difficult to analyse the impression he made on her, but she could understand why he made those round him laugh and why some of the gentlemen on the opposite side of the table kept asking:

"What do you think about that, Leo? I have been waiting for your opinion."

The gentlemen were obviously prepared to value what he said and to include him in their conversations, but the women, she realised, talked to him in a very different way.

It was almost as if there was an open invitation in their eyes, and she told herself scornfully that it was an invitation he would seldom, if ever, refuse.

They had sat down to dinner with almost equal numbers of male and female guests; but after dinner when they had left the Dining-Room for a large and very beautiful Salon, it was mostly men who arrived.

There were large French windows opening out onto a terrace from which there were steps leading down to a formal garden.

There was no wind and the night was warm.

The ladies pulled light scarves over their décolletages and moved across the lawns, which were edged with fairy-lights, and walked under trees hung with Chinese lanterns.

A fountain was playing in the centre of the garden and it was lit in some clever way so that the water rising towards the sky was tinged with gold.

It was all very romantic and Yola found herself walking beside the Prince Napoleon.

"Tell me about yourself," he said. "You must realise that because you are so beautiful, after tonight all Paris will want to talk to you, and it is doubtful if I shall get another chance."

He spoke with the complacent conceit of a man to whom women were all too easy a prey.

"My life is not particularly interesting, Sir," Yola answered, "but I would love to hear about yours. My father used to read me your speeches, and when you spoke of democracy, I thought it was a clarion call to the country which has moved away from it lately."

The Prince Napoleon looked surprised.

"I did not expect my speeches to be read or appreciated by somebody as lovely as yourself."

"I think you under-rate your importance, Sir."

He looked at her now in a different way.

"So you are a woman of brains as well as beauty!" he said. "A devastating combination!"

"I hope you are right," Yola replied, smiling.

He bent towards her and she thought he was going to say something that would be particularly intimate, but at that moment Aimée came to his side.

"Forgive me, Sir," she said, "but the Ambassador from the Vatican has just arrived and is particularly anxious to have a word with you. I promised to plead his cause for him."

As the Prince was somewhat reluctantly listening to Aimée, Yola heard a voice on her other side say:

"You are certainly starting your progress in Paris in a Royal manner!"

There was an unmistakably mocking note in the Marquis's voice, and as she turned towards him, to her surprise he took her arm and moved her away from the Prince and into the shadow of some white lilac bushes.

Before she could protest, he said:

"Aimée does not think the Prince a suitable person with whom you should start your acquaintance with Paris."

"But why?" Yola asked in a deliberately innocent

voice, well aware of the reason why Aimée was disengaging her from the Prince.

"She considers me a more reputable guide," the Marquis answered. "So, first of all, I would like to ask you, *Mademoiselle* Lefleur, if you will let me take you driving tomorrow morning?"

"Did Aimée tell you we were free?" she enquired.

"Aimée, much as I love her, is not included in the invitation. My chaise is a small one and there is only room for two."

Yola hesitated.

She did not wish to seem over-eager, but she knew it would be an opportunity to talk to the Marquis and find out a little about him.

"Silence means consent," the Marquis said. "I will call for you at ten o'clock."

"I think actually I have a previous engagement to drive with Aimée in the Bois."

"I will take you. I am quite prepared to sacrifice myself to the fashion parade, if that is what you wish."

"If I have a choice," Yola said, "I would rather see a little of Paris."

"It is true that you have not been here before?"

"Of course. You heard Aimée say so."

"Then how can you manage to look as you do?" he asked.

Yola did not reply, and he added:

"Do you realise that every woman who is here tonight will be hammering on Worth's door tomorrow long before he is awake and calling him every name under the sun?"

"Why?" Yola questioned.

"You do not need me to tell you why," he said. "Your gown is sensational; but then, I have a feeling that anything you wear looks different from the way it would on any other woman."

Yola did not answer, and the Marquis asked suddenly:

"Who are you? How can you have appeared like a meteor from outer space to confound us all?"

"Do you really want an answer to that question?" Yola enquired.

"I not only want one, I intend to have one!" the Marquis answered. "And when I am determined on getting something I want, I assure you I am always successful!"

Chapter Four

"It is beautiful!" Yola exclaimed as they drove along the wide Boulevards and into the Place de la Concorde.

"It is a transformation," the Marquis agreed, "from a half-mediaeval city of slums and narrow streets. And the Emperor's vision has been amazingly well carried out by Baron Haussman."

He spoke with a note of admiration in his voice which made Yola say almost involuntarily:

"You sound as if you admire the Emperor."

"I certainly admire him for what he has achieved," the Marquis replied.

"And as a man?"

The Marquis smiled as he said:

"I think I will leave you to judge His Majesty for yourself, for you will undoubtedly meet him while you are in Paris."

"Why should you think that?" Yola asked.

The Marquis smiled again, and she thought it was with mockery.

"The way you appeared last night, and the envy of the women besides the admiration of the men, has doubtless been related to the Emperor over his *petit déjeuner.*"

"I think you are flattering me," Yola said.

"I shall think you are being a hypocrite," the Marquis retorted, "if you protest that I am not telling the truth."

They drove on, and while Yola was admiring the new buildings, the sparkling fountains, and the almost breathtaking magnificence of the Champs Élysées, her thoughts were really concentrated on the Marquis.

She had thought last night that he was nothing but the pleasure-seeking man-about-town she had expected him to be.

Although he had tried to talk to her quietly in the garden, they had been interrupted every moment by women inviting him to their houses, to parties, to *tête-à-têtes,* all determined in fact to alert his attemtion to themselves.

'That is what he enjoys,' Yola had thought scornfully, and she had gone to bed feeling certain that her opinion of him was exactly what she had expected it to be.

But somehow this morning he seemed different.

As he showed her Paris, driving with an expertise which, as an expert herself, she had to admire, there was a serious note in his voice that had not been there previously.

"There is so much of Paris I would like to show you," he said, "not only the splendours of the new Opera House and the Tuileries Palace, but also the Paris of the people, such as the Dance-Halls where the shop-girls gather, which have the spontaneous gaiety that you will not find at Society parties."

"I would like to see that side of Paris," Yola replied.

"Do you really mean that?" he asked. "I was only suggesting it to see your reaction. I am quite certain you would find it extremely boring."

"Why should you think that?" she asked sharply.

"Because it is, I am sure, unlike anything you have ever known before," he answered.

"You are assuming a great deal about me which may be untrue," Yola protested.

"Then tell me the truth."

She did not reply and after a moment he said:

"You are being very enigmatic and mysterious. Is that a pose, or is there a reason for it?"

"I think that question is very impolite," Yola replied.

The Marquis laughed.

"I did not mean it to be. I am just interested in you."

Yola longed to retort: "As you are interested in so many other ladies." But instead she replied demurely:

"I am well aware how honoured I am that you spend so much time with me and express so much interest."

"Now you are being sarcastic."

"But, as you would say . . . it is the truth. Even in the country we have the newspapers, and I see your name amongst those who are present at every notable occasion."

"May I ask why you are interested in me?" the Marquis enquired.

Yola realised she had been a little indiscreet and replied quickly:

"I have always been interested in Aimée's friends and she has mentioned you when she was talking of the different people she knows."

"Aimée is an exceptionally clever woman," the Marquis said. "No-one else could carry off her position with such *élan* and such dignity."

He paused; then, turning his face for a moment to look at Yola, he said:

"Is that what you want too? A Salon and a protector as wealthy and distinguished as the *Duc*?"

Just for a second Yola thought his question was insulting.

Then she remembered that, considering her reddened lips, her driving alone with a man after such a short acquaintance, and being a friend of Aimée, there was only one construction he could put on her behaviour.

It was what she had wanted and what she had set out to achieve.

At the same time, it gave her a shock, and not a pleasant one, to know what he was thinking, and after a moment she said:

"I have not . . . yet decided my . . . future."

"You have an alternative to taking Paris by storm?"

"I could . . . marry."

"I should imagine that is certainly a possibility," the Marquis agreed, "and I have the feeling that that is why you have come to Paris, to decide whether to say yes or no."

He was surprisingly perceptive, Yola thought, and, after a moment she replied:

"I do not want to talk about myself. Tell me more of what Paris was like before half of it was pulled down."

"Does it really interest you," the Marquis asked, "that in 1851 there were only eight miles of underground sewers to accommodate the city, and unsanitary conditions resulted in an abnormal number of deaths?"

Again he was mocking her, but Yola merely laughed.

"Strange though it may seem, I am interested," she answered. "I have read quite a number of books which describe what Paris was like in the eighteenth century, and the manner in which the poor people lived appals me!"

"For many of them, conditions are not much better today," the Marquis said. "Now, let me see, that elegant gown you were wearing last night must have cost all of sixteen hundred francs, while seamstresses earn on an average three francs a week!"

"You are trying to make me feel uncomfortable," Yola said accusingly, "and if women like myself did not order gowns, there would be hundreds of seamstresses out of work."

They sparred with each other in a manner which she found strangely exciting until the Marquis took her back to the Rue du Faubourg Saint-Honoré.

As they drew up at the front door he asked:

"Will you dine with me tonight?"

Yola hesitated.

She wanted to accept his invitation. At the same

time, she did not want him to think she was grabbing at him as obviously as many other women did.

Then she told herself that it was not of the least consequence what the Marquis thought of her behaviour.

She had very nearly made up her mind that she would not marry him; and once she was certain of her decision, the quicker she returned to the Castle to face the tussle with her grandmother, the better.

"Thank you," she said. "Am I to come *très chic* or are you taking me to dance in the slums?"

"I will do that another night," the Marquis replied, "but this evening I want to talk to you."

"What about?"

"Need you ask?" he replied, with a twist of his lips. "And because I really mean to talk, I shall not take you to the Café Anglais or anywhere that is large and crowded, but instead we will dine at the Grand Vefour. If you do not already know what it is like, ask Aimée."

When Yola did in fact ask Aimée about the Grand Vefour, Aimée clapped her hands.

"So he has planned an intimate dinner with you!" she exclaimed. "That is exactly what we want. Now you will be able to judge for yourself what he is really like. It is impossible in a room crowded with other people or when he is occupied with his horses."

Aimée then told Yola that the Grand Vefour was in the Palais Royal, which the *Duc* d'Orleans, who had been partly responsible for the Revolution, had turned into a place of shops, restaurants, and gambling-dens, to become overnight the richest man in France.

"The Grand Vefour is interesting because it has remained exactly as it was at the time of the Revolution," Aimée said. "The food is superlative, and it is where people go when they want to be alone with each other."

"What shall I wear?" Yola asked.

Needless to say, such an important feminine subject occupied their minds for a long time.

When finally Yola entered the Salon where the Marquis was waiting for her, she was wearing one of Pierre Floret's gowns, which became her even more than the one she had worn the night before.

It was far simpler, and the pale leaf-green colour made her skin look like velvet and was reflected in her eyes.

Again, the gown was swept to the back in a cascade of tiny frills, while from the front Yola looked like a nymph rising from the Seine.

She felt a strange excitement at the thought of the evening ahead, but there was also a glint of apprehension in her eyes, because she had never before dined alone with a man, and it seemed such an outrageous thing to do that she was afraid of her own daring.

The Marquis, incredibly elegant and perhaps, Yola thought, not quite so mocking as usual, stood for a moment looking at her as she entered the room.

Then he walked towards her to take her hand in his and raise it to his lips.

"A million men must have told you that you are very beautiful," he said, "and as the million-and-first, I can only say that it is a very inadequate adjective."

"I realise you have had a lot of practice in saying such delightful things," Yola answered, "but I admit to listening to them with satisfaction."

"Why?" the Marquis asked.

"Because I was afraid that I should feel insignificant in Paris. Everything I had heard about it was so overwhelming that I expected just to slip into the corner like a little country mouse and go completely unnoticed."

"And instead?" he questioned.

"I find myself dining with the most talked-about gentleman in *Haute Société*," Yola replied.

She meant to be provocative; she meant, if possible, to needle him a little; but, to her surprise, he threw back his head and laughed.

"Marvellous!" he exclaimed. "I am sure you thought all that out in your bath!"

To her annoyance, Yola felt herself flush because that was exactly what she had done.

"Now that you have said your piece," the Marquis went on, "let me tell you that you are very lovely and it is positively a crime that I am taking you somewhere where for want of a larger audience you will have to shine only for me."

"You warned me," Yola replied, "and I suppose if I had insisted you would have taken me to the Café Anglais."

"There is still time for you to change your mind," he answered.

She had the feeling that as he spoke he was quite certain that she should not do so, and it irritated her to think that he should be so sure of himself.

He was too complacently aware that most women would prefer to be alone with him rather than to receive the plaudits of a crowd.

"Aimée tells me that the food at the Grand Vefour is superlative, and actually I am rather hungry," Yola said.

She turned towards the door as she spoke, and she heard him laugh softly behind her as if he was not deceived.

There was a closed carriage waiting outside; there were two men on the box wearing the Montereau livery, and again the horses were superb.

It suddenly struck Yola that the Marquis's way of life must be a very expensive one. In which case, she asked herself, who was paying for it?

Her grandmother had said that the Montereau family was impoverished after the Revolution, and she had heard her father say that the Marquis's father and mother had lived in a frugal way in a small house on the outskirts of Paris.

She was certain that the reason the Marquis had as a boy stayed at Beauharnais Castle was that after his father died his mother was left impoverished and her grandfather had been sorry for her.

At the Castle there had been horses to ride and

tutors to teach the boy Marquis, which could not otherwise have been afforded.

So where did this opulence come from now? Yola wondered, and thought contemptuously that the Marquis must be financed by the women who loved him.

The idea revolted her and she thought that even to eat a dinner that had been paid for by another woman was too degrading to contemplate.

As if he sensed her sudden stiffness and withdrawal into herself, the Marquis leaned back in a corner of the carriage and regarded her with twinkling eyes.

"What is upsetting you?"

"How do you know there is anything?" Yola enquired coldly.

"You have very expressive eyes," he answered. "I have always been told that the eyes mirror the soul, but yours reveal your thoughts, your feelings, and the impulses of your heart."

"If you are trying to make me afraid that you are reading my thoughts," Yola replied, "let me inform you, *Monsieur*, that nevertheless I shall keep my secrets."

"I refuse to allow you to call me *Monsieur*," the Marquis retorted. "I am Leo to you, as you are Yola to me. Shall I tell you why?"

"Yes," Yola replied, trying not to sound curious.

"Because we are starting out on a voyage of discovery," he answered. "We are going to learn a lot about each other, you and I, and the first thing to do is to clear the decks of anything that is superfluous or inhibitive."

Yola looked startled.

It was strange to hear that he should want to discover things about her as she did about him.

Then she told herself that it was the sort of flirtatious comment that any man in the Marquis's position would make to a woman who was dining alone with him.

She only wished she had more experience of other men to judge him by.

Having known so few men and certainly never having dined unchaperoned with one, it was hard, she thought, to determine when the Marquis was speaking the truth and when he was merely using his far-fabled charm on her in the same way he used it on other women.

The Grand Vefour was certainly conducive to intimacy.

It was very small, and the walls and ceiling were painted with the same design of flowers and fruit as they had been when it first opened.

There were only a few red plush sofas in each of the two rooms, and they were set so discreetly apart from the other diners that it was impossible for a low-voiced conversation to be overheard.

Yola looked round with delight.

The place was a part of history, and she wondered how many of the great persons who had figured in the Revolution had seen their reflections in the mirrors as she could see hers or had eaten a good meal before they went either to their own deaths or to the deaths of their enemies.

The Marquis was obviously a very welcome guest and they were shown with much bowing and scraping to a table in the corner of the room.

Yola was presented with a large hand-written menu, but she merely closed it and said to the Marquis:

"Will you choose for me? I would like, please, to eat one of their specialties."

It was inevitable that there should be a long discussion about the various dishes and then the wine, and Yola waited until the Marquis, having finished, turned sideways to look at her.

"Well?" he asked.

"Well what?" she queried in reply.

"What is your conclusion about me? I have seen in your eyes a variety of expressions, most of them critical."

"Why should you think I am critical?" Yola parried.

"It is not only what I see but what I feel," he said. "When we first talked for a brief moment last night, I had the feeling you were fencing with me."

Yola looked away across the room, so that he would not see the startled expression in her eyes.

"Where I am concerned," the Marquis went on, "there is really no need for you to say anything. I find that I know what you are thinking and feeling, and this intrigues me as I have never before been intrigued."

"I do not . . . think that is . . . true," Yola said, finding it hard to know how to reply.

"It is a waste of time to protest against something which you know as well as I do is completely true," the Marquis retorted. "So, I repeat my question of last night—who are you and where do you come from?"

"As you are so perceptive, there should be no need for me to answer you in words," Yola said.

"How shall I try to hold a piece of quicksilver in my hand?" the Marquis asked. "But let me tell you this—before I met you, I would have been prepared to wager quite a considerable sum of money that it would be impossible for me not to know within a few hours of her acquaintance a great deal about a woman, any woman."

He paused before he went on in a lower voice:

"With you it is quite different. There is something I do not understand, something to which I cannot put a name, and yet it is unquestionably there."

"Then perhaps your 'voyage of discovery' will take a little longer than you anticipated."

"It can take as long as you permit. I am in no hurry."

"But I am," Yola answered. "I intend to spend a very short time in Paris."

"Then you think your problem will soon be answered—to marry, or not to marry."

"I was almost certain I had the answer before I arrived."

The Marquis looked at her for a long moment before he said:

"And now you are uncertain: why?"

Because she was afraid that he was being too intuitive, Yola merely shrugged her shoulders and replied:

"Perhaps Aimée has made me envious."

The Marquis was silent for a moment before he said:

"Could you really contemplate joining *les expertes des sciences galantes—les grandes cocottes* of Paris, who are undoubtedly one of the show-pieces of the city?"

Yola quickly told herself that she must not be insulted by his question or by the fact that his view of Aimée's position was rather different from how she herself visualised it.

She tried to find words in which to reply, but then she heard him laugh softly to himself as he said:

"I may be wrong, but something tells me that you have no intention of entering the half-world of which I have spoken. If this is so, why are you dressed as you are? And why the quite unnecessary crimson on your lips?"

Yola drew in her breath.

She was afraid that the Marquis with his uncanny perception could penetrate her disguise, but then she told herself that such fears were ridiculous.

Even if he suspected that she was not as sophisticated as she was trying to appear, he could have no idea that he was talking to the girl who might in the future become his wife.

"I told you I was afraid I would appear as a country mouse in the glittering splendour of Paris," she said.

"Country mice do not look like you!" the Marquis answered. "But, like a little mouse, Yola, you are trying to evade me, to slip away, and prevent me from capturing you. Your efforts to escape, let me tell you, will be quite useless."

Yola was saved from replying, because at that moment the first course he had ordered arrived.

It was in fact delicious, but somehow her hunger had gone and instead she had a strange feeling in her throat which made it hard to swallow.

She drank a little champagne and thought it gave her a gaiety that made their conversation sparkle like the wine itself.

While they were eating the Marquis made her laugh, but though he was occasionally scathing about the people he knew, he was also witty with his turns of phrases that would have amused her father.

'I can understand why Papa liked him,' she thought. 'At the same time, Papa could not have known that the Marquis had become such a Socialite.'

Her father had never cared for city life and had been content to stay at the Castle, except when occasionally he travelled, usually, Yola knew, so that he could be with *Madame* Renazé.

But seeing the Marquis so smartly and meticulously dressed, and knowing that the wit which made her laugh was what endeared him to the people who had applauded him last night, she could not imagine him in the quiet of the Castle.

'No,' she thought, 'here he has his own niche in which he glitters almost as if he were a leading actor upon a stage, and he would hate to be overshadowed by the Castle, which through the years has seen a thousand men like him come and go.'

At the same time, she had to admit, although she hated to do so, that he had a fascination that was unmistakable.

When the meal was over and there was only their coffee left in front of them, the Marquis sat back with a glass of brandy in his hand and said:

"Now, let us continue our conversation where we left off. Too much seriousness at meal-times is conducive to indigestion."

"I have not come to Paris to be serious," Yola flashed in reply.

"As you are making a decision that will affect

your whole life, nothing could be more serious or more fundamentally important," the Marquis contradicted. "Tell me about this man—is he in love with you?"

He did not wait for Yola's reply but added:

"Of course he is! He is wildly, crazily, head-over-heels in love, and you are everything that he has ever looked for and longed to find in the woman he would marry."

There was a note in his voice which made Yola feel he was being too intimate, but before she could answer, the Marquis went on:

"Are you in love with him?"

Yola shook her head.

"Then there is your answer!"

"Why?"

"Because a marriage without love can be a hell on earth!"

"Most young people in France have their marriages arranged for them," Yola replied.

"Most women are not as sensitive as you are," he answered. "Could you really contemplate living with a man if you did not care for him, if he did not mean something very special that no other man could mean?"

"That is what I . . . thought . . . myself," Yola said, almost as if the words were forced from her. "At the same time, what is the . . . alternative?"

"Not what you are pretending to contemplate," the Marquis replied sharply. "You should wait until you fall in love."

"And suppose that never happens? After all, it is only in story-books that there is the inevitable happy ending."

The Marquis reached out and took her hand.

"Shall I tell your fortune?" he asked. "Shall I tell you that you are like the Sleeping Beauty, unawakened, unaware as yet of what love can mean? One day you will know, and then you will realise that nothing else in the whole world is of any consequence."

Yola was so startled at the serious way in which

the Marquis spoke that she stared at him. Then as his eyes held hers she hastily glanced away, afraid of what he might read in her expression.

With a tremendous effort she forced herself to say:

"How do you know that I have not... already been in... love... or am not... in love at this... moment?"

"You could not deceive me," the Marquis replied.

"I am not trying to do so. I am merely saying that you are assuming a great many things with which I am not prepared to agree."

"Look at me, Yola."

She wanted to refuse, but somehow without her conscious volition she found herself looking into his eyes, and his face was close to hers.

"I could swear," he said very quickly, "swear on everything that I hold holy, that you have not only never been in love but that no man has ever touched you."

His words were a shock to Yola and she felt her fingers quiver as he still held her hand in his, and it was impossible to prevent the colour from rising into her pale cheeks.

"I knew I was not mistaken," the Marquis said, and there was a note of triumph in his voice.

Yola snatched her hand away from his.

"I think it is time we left."

"Of course," the Marquis agreed.

He called for the bill. Then, as he put over her shoulders the green velvet wrap which matched her gown, he asked:

"Where would you like to go?"

She was just about to reply that she did not know, when a man came from the inner room and walked towards their table.

As he reached them she looked up and realised it was the Prince Napoleon.

"*Mademoiselle* Lefleur," he said, "I am enchanted to see you again."

He kissed her hand, then said to the Marquis:

"I might have guessed, Leo, that you would be one step ahead of me. In fact, I asked the adorable Aimée last night if *Mademoiselle* was free to dine with me, but she said that she was engaged."

The Prince threw out his hands with a theatrical gesture.

"Leo—it is always Leo!" he said to Yola. "One night I, or some other frustrated gentleman, will drown him in the Seine!"

"Could you be so cruel?" Yola asked.

"To him? Certainly!" the Prince replied. "To you? Never!"

"We were just leaving," the Marquis said.

"Then I will tell you what I will do," the Prince said. "I will take you both to a party being given by a friend of mine. It will amuse *Mademoiselle* Lefleur, and of course, Leo, she will be exceedingly pleased to welcome you."

"Whom are you talking about?" the Marquis enquired.

"Who else but the entrancing La Païva?" the Prince replied.

Despite herself Yola stiffened.

She had learnt, from the girls at school, the names of the famous Courtesans of Paris, and she knew that La Païva was the most important of them all.

Her jewels were described and acclaimed in every newspaper, and her house in the Champs Élysées, which had been built by her millionaire German lover, was so fantastic that the reporters almost ran out of superlatives to describe it.

Yola had read of La Païva's solid onyx bath with its sculptured gilt taps set with jewels.

Yola knew of the opulent glory in which she appeared at Longchamps Races, at first nights, and at the Opera, and that her box in the Théâtre des Italiens faced the Imperial Box.

Whatever else was left unrecorded in the French newspapers, La Païva had columns written about her day after day, week after week, and in this year of the International Exhibition more than one writer had asked who in fact could be more magnificent and more entrancingly Parisian than La Païva.

At the same time, Yola was well aware that La Païva symbolised the *demi-mondaines*, of whom *Madame* Renazé and Aimée had spoken so scathingly.

As *Madame* had said, both she and Aimée were a true second wife to a man, and they would not soil their lips with that ordinary name which described La Païva and her type.

Yola was about to tell the Prince that she had no intention of going to a party given by such a woman, but the Marquis said it for her.

"Your Imperial Highness is very gracious," he replied, "and I thank you, Sir, for thinking of us, but unfortunately *Mademoiselle* and I have a previous engagement."

"You have?" the Prince enquired. "Where?"

"With some friends, Sir, who are expecting us after dinner. We have promised to join them and we would not wish them to be disappointed."

The Prince gave a shrug of his shoulders as if he accepted defeat, then he said:

"If they do not keep you late, come and join me, even if only for half an hour."

He did not wait for the Marquis's reply, but took Yola's hand in both of his and said:

"I want you to come. I want to see you again, and there is so much I want to say to you."

He was speaking in a manner which no-one, however young or innocent, could misunderstand, and as Yola looked at him uncertainly, the Prince said softly:

"Last night I lost my heart. You cannot be so cruel as not to allow me to tell you about it."

"Your Imperial Highness is very gracious, but as the Marquis has already said, we have a previous engagement."

"Why not let him go alone and you come with

me?" the Prince asked. "I assure you he will not be lonely for long."

"That I can well believe," Yola answered. "But I am sure Your Imperial Highness would not wish me to appear impolite to my friends."

"Quite frankly, I am not in the least interested how you appear to them," the Prince replied. "All I want is for you to be polite, and perhaps a little more, to me!"

There was a glint in his eyes which told Yola that he would be prepared to fight to get his own way, but she took her hand from his and said:

"I am sorry, *Monsieur*."

"It would be some consolation if I believed you really were," the Prince answered, "but I shall hope to see you tomorrow. Perhaps you will dine with me?"

Yola drew in her breath, but again the Marquis stepped in.

"It is unfortunate, Sir, but I have arranged to take the *Duc*, Aimée, and *Mademoiselle* to the Theatre."

The Prince glared at the Marquis and it was obvious that he suspected that this was not the truth.

"Curse you, Leo! This is not the first time you have proved obstructive, and quite frankly I resent it!"

"I can only regret, Sir, that you should think it is anything personal," the Marquis said. "It is just that *Mademoiselle*'s visit to Paris is such a short one and a full programme has already been arranged for her."

"Then it can be cancelled!" the Prince said, almost spitting out the words. "And make no mistake, I shall see that it is!"

Once again he took Yola's hand in his.

"You are fascinating and quite irresistible," he said, "and I assure you that I shall not give up easily."

He kissed her hand, his lips lingering on the softness of her skin. Then with a baleful glance at the Marquis he walked back to the inner room from which he had come, leaving them alone.

The Marquis put his hand under Yola's elbow and said:

"The sooner we get out of here, the better!"

The carriage was outside and as she stepped into it Yola told herself that had the Marquis not been there she would have felt afraid.

The Prince had somehow been overpowering, and it was obvious that because he was Royal he thought it presumptuous of the Marquis to interfere and unheard of for her not to accede immediately to his request.

As the door shut and the horses started off, Yola said nervously:

"Will he make . . . trouble for you?"

"Are you thinking of me?"

"Of course," she replied. "And thank you for protecting me. I realised that that was what you were doing."

"You are quite sure you would not have liked to accept the Prince's invitation? After all, he is a very important man."

"I have no . . . wish to be . . . alone with the . . . Prince."

She made an effort to speak calmly, but there was a perceptible quiver on the word "alone," which the Marquis did not miss.

"This sort of life is not for you," he said sharply.

Yola did not answer, and he asked:

"How old are you?"

The question was sharp, and because she had not expected it Yola found herself stammering over what she and Aimée had agreed she should say.

"I am . . . t-twenty-two . . . nearly t-twenty-three."

"I do not believe it!"

Yola was silent and after a moment the Marquis went on:

"I will believe it if you tell me you have stepped straight out of a Convent and have seen nothing of men and women or of the world—any sort of world.

Otherwise, I know irrefutably that you are much younger."

"I have always been told," Yola said in a small voice, "that it is rude to discuss a lady's age."

"The number of years is not really the point," the Marquis said. "It is what you feel and who you are that counts, and I know in my heart that you are little more than a child and are quite incapable of dealing with a man like the Prince!"

"Then I shall not . . . deal with . . . him. He cannot . . . force me to be . . . with him."

"He will use every weapon in his power to get what he wants," the Marquis said. "No-one refuses his advances—no woman! He will hunt you as the huntsman does his prey, until he captures you."

Yola gave an involuntary little cry, then she said:

"You are trying to . . . frighten me. No-one can make me accept the . . . advances of the Prince. I think he is . . . horrible!"

"You would rather be with me?"

Before she could think, Yola told the truth.

"Much rather."

"That is what I want to hear. And do not be afraid—I will see that the Prince does not frighten you."

"But what could he . . . do to you?" Yola asked apprehensively.

"He can make himself very unpleasant," the Marquis said with a serious note in his voice, "but I think he is unlikely to do so. If people ask the reason for his enmity and learn we have fallen out over a woman, it would damage his reputation as a 'lady-killer'!"

"I hope you are . . . right," Yola said nervously.

"Let us forget about him."

The Marquis put his arm along the back of the seat so that it was behind her.

"Let us forget he ever happened," he said in a beguiling tone. "Instead, I want to tell you what I have felt tonight since we have been alone together."

There was a different tone in his voice and Yola

thought suddenly that in a way the Marquis was even more dangerous than the Prince had been.

She knew he was going to make love to her, and because she was afraid of her own feelings, was uncertain and bewildered, she said involuntarily:

"No!"

"Why do you say it like that?" the Marquis asked.

"Because I do not . . . want you to . . . say what I . . . think you intend to . . . say."

"So you are as perceptive about me as I am about you?"

"Only in this . . . I think."

"You knew I was going to tell you how much you attract me, how I have been thinking about you ever since you made that dramatic entrance last night, skilfully thought out by you and Aimée."

Yola looked at him in a startled manner, then realised he was very near to her.

The new gas-lights installed by Baron Haussman flashed on the Marquis's face as the carriage passed them, and the expression in his eyes made her heart give a sudden leap.

"You know without my telling you," the Marquis said, "that I want to kiss you more than I have ever wanted anything in my whole life."

"No!" Yola said again, turning her head towards the window.

The Marquis looked at her profile for a moment, then asked very softly:

"How many men have kissed you already?"

Yola did not answer, and after a moment he said:

"You do not really have to answer that question. Oh, my dear, you are very transparent. It is like looking into a clear stream—quite the most intriguing thing I have ever done!"

"I think I should . . . go home," Yola said a little nervously.

"I have told the carriage to drive to the Bois," the Marquis replied. "There is something I want to show you when it is not crowded by the world of fashion and when even the nightingales can be heard in the silence."

Yola felt that if she was wise she would protest that she wished to go home at once.

But instead she moved a little farther into the corner of the carriage, and she realised that the Marquis was no longer encroaching upon her.

He had taken his arm from behind her and was merely looking at her, but because she was afraid of the expression in his eyes she dared not look back at him.

It took only a short time for the carriage to reach the Bois, and as there seemed to be little to say, they sat in silence.

Yet, Yola had the strange feeling that they spoke to each other without words.

As the carriage came to a standstill the footman jumped down to open the door and the Marquis stepped out to help her alight.

He took her hand in his and put it on his arm, then drew her along a little path through the woods. It wound in and out amongst the trees until they came to a small rock-garden.

It was one of the attractive innovations arranged on the Emperor's instructions, and it had changed the wild forest that had been full of robbers and footpads into an oasis of beauty.

Yola remembered someone saying that it could only have been accomplished "by the hand of an enchanter," and that was what she felt now when she saw what the Marquis had brought her to see.

There was a small waterfall cascading down into a pool and the moonlight coming through the clouds turned it into burnished silver.

Then it wound in a rippling stream between banks of azaleas and spring flowers.

They were all in bloom and the fragrance of them filled the night air.

It was almost like a child's garden, for everything was in miniature and it had a fairy-tale quality which made Yola think of the Castle and the places where she had played when she was young.

She stood gazing at the loveliness of it. Then she heard the Marquis say quietly:

"I brought you here because tonight you look like a nymph, a nymph from the cascade; like a water-sprite who enchants and bemuses a mere man, yet ripples away from him so that he finds it hard to capture her."

There was something in the way he spoke and in the depth of his voice that made Yola feel as if she vibrated to every word.

Then as if she could not prevent herself she turned her head and the moonlight was on his face.

There was an expression in his eyes that she had never seen before and it made him look different, and yet in some strange way familiar, as if she had known him long, long ago and had now found him again.

Just for a moment they stood looking at each other, with only the sound of the cascade to break the silence. Then the Marquis's arms went round her.

He drew her very slowly into his arms, and although Yola knew she ought to prevent him from touching her, she was somehow magnetised into doing what he wished.

He looked down into her eyes and then his lips were on hers.

It was the first time that Yola had ever been kissed, and she had never imagined that a man's lips could be so possessive.

She felt as if he not only held her captive but took her will from her, so that she ceased to be herself and instead became a part of him.

She tried to define to herself what she was feeling, but his kiss was all part of the music of the water, the fragrance of the flowers, and the wonder of the moonlight.

It was so perfect, so romantic, so everything she thought a kiss should be.

Then he held her closer and his lips became more insistent, more demanding.

She told herself that he was drawing her heart from her body and that somehow she should prevent him from doing so.

Chapter Five

"It is really tremendously exciting!" Yola exclaimed.

Her eyes were sparkling and her lips smiling as she moved from exhibit to exhibit in the International Exhibition.

The Marquis had driven her there in his open chaise, and she was thrilled from the moment they stepped into the enormous glass and iron building in the Champ de Mars on the Left Bank of the Seine.

There were fairgrounds and an Imperial Pavilion which was an Oriental concept carried out with striped awnings and a multitude of golden eagles.

But the majority of the exhibits could be found in the Palais de l'Industrie and the different National Pavilions.

England was presenting a Bible Society kiosk, a Protestant Church, a model farm, and machines for agriculture.

The Marquis laughed at it.

"Nothing could show more clearly," he said to Yola, "the social and spiritual chasm which divides Victorian England from the Second Empire of France."

It was the sort of remark that her father would have made, and Yola fancied that the Marquis was testing her to see if she understood what he was trying to say.

"There is no lack of the exotic," she murmured demurely, "if that is what you are looking for."

They had already seen the Morocco tents, the Turkish Mosque, and the Moslem sarcophagus. They had also visited the bamboo house from Japan and seen a porcelain pagoda in the garden presented by China.

"I want to know what you think of this," the Marquis said.

Yola saw that he was pointing out a fifty-eight-ton steel gun manufactured by Krupp of Essen and displayed in the Prussian section.

As Yola stared at it he said:

"It is capable of firing a thousand-pound shell, and the French newspapers regard it with a great deal of ironic amusement."

Yola looked at him before she said:

"But you are taking it seriously."

"I think if it was directed against us it could be very serious indeed," the Marquis replied.

He moved Yola on to where there was an exhibit of a graceful new rifle, the *chassepot*.

"Is that the only weapon we have on show?" Yola asked in a low voice.

"There is a relief map of our forts," the Marquis replied, "which, last time I was here, was being studied with concentrated interest by a number of Prussian officers."

Yola knew exactly what he was trying to say, and she felt a little shiver of fear in case those who talked of France going to war might prove to be right.

The preceding year the Austrians had suffered an unexpected defeat at the battle of Sadowa and the event had marked the emergence of Prussia as a military power.

Yola remembered how her father had said that the French would never tolerate the Germans menacing them on their frontiers.

Then she told herself that she was being needlessly apprehensive.

The whole country was at the moment intoxicated with pleasure and pride—pride in its machinery and its spectacular Army, and pleasure in its money and its beautiful Capital.

"There will be peace in the future," Yola murmured almost to herself.

"I wish we could be sure of that," the Marquis replied.

Then with a change of mood which she knew was characteristic of him, he swept her away to admire the French Food Courts where every wine-district had its own exhibit and cellar.

"There is so much to see!" Yola said with a sigh after they had been walking for hours. "I keep feeling we must come to the end, only to discover there are hundreds more things I want to see and admire."

They found it difficult to make a decision as to where to eat.

"There are two miles of cafés and restaurants," the Marquis said. "You can eat and drink in every language. Which shall it be?"

It was in fact a very difficult choice.

In the Spanish restaurant, the waitresses, with their rich olive complexions, straight eye-brows, and round eyes, wore purple satin skirts, white lace shawls, and high combs and damask roses in their raven-black hair.

Yola had almost decided to eat there, but then they peeped into the Russian café, where the waitresses were blonde and wore elaborate diadems with ribbons floating behind.

"One place we will avoid," the Marquis said firmly, "is the English Tavern. The girls wear very unbecoming clothes and I am told the food is dreadful!"

In the end, because they felt it would be amusing they ate in the Tunisian café, where there were girls with slanting almond-shaped eyes framed in khol.

"I know one thing," Yola said when they had finished, and had laughed all the way through the meal, "when in France one should eat with the French."

"When in France you should do everything with the French!" the Marquis replied. "And that applies to love."

There was a note in his voice which made Yola feel shy.

There had been so much to see and do at the Exhibition that there had been no chance of speaking intimately.

But she was vividly conscious of what had occurred the night before and that she had gone to sleep thinking of him and had awakened to find his name on her lips.

She could still feel the sensations he had aroused in her, and she knew that because they were together she felt a strange excitement she had never known before, and it affected everything she said and did.

"I am not in love!" she tried to tell herself, but she knew that she was lying.

They spent another hour in the afternoon looking at more exhibits, and then because the Marquis said he thought she was tired they found his chaise and drove back towards Aimée's house.

"You are dining with me this evening," the Marquis said, "and then I shall have a chance to talk to you."

There was a groom perched up behind them on a small seat, and although it was unlikely that he could overhear what they were saying, his mere presence made it impossible for them to talk intimately.

"Are you asking me or commanding me?" Yola enquired.

"I am asking you—begging you, if you like," the Marquis replied, "but I shall not allow you to say no."

Yola had no wish to refuse his invitation.

At the same time, she felt that she was becoming more and more deeply involved with him and she was not quite certain what she should do about it.

She had wanted to get to know him, to find out what he was like; but now she felt as if everything was happening too quickly and it was impossible to think and almost as hard to breathe.

"Thank you for taking me to the Exhibition," she said conventionally.

"It was like taking a child to her first Pantomime," the Marquis said with a smile.

"Are you really so blasé?" Yola retorted. "The French Exhibition should make you feel very proud."

"I found it difficult to look at anything except the person I was with."

Yola was well aware that the Marquis's eyes had been on her almost the whole time they had been going round the Exhibition, and she had deliberately not looked at him because she was half-afraid of what he was saying without words.

"I think we have talked enough about *La Belle France*," the Marquis said as they neared the Rue du Faubourg Saint-Honoré. "This evening I intend to talk about you—and of course about myself."

"Supposing Aimée has arranged a party for me?" Yola suggested.

"I have already told her that we are dining together."

"Before you asked me?"

"I told you that I would not allow you to refuse me."

"You are being very dictatorial."

Yola spoke lightly. At the same time, she felt almost as if she was struggling against him, that he was encroaching upon her, overwhelming her before she was really ready for it.

"I think I have a right to be dictatorial," the Marquis replied to her accusation, "and a great many other things as well, but I will tell you about that this evening. Be ready for me at seven-thirty."

As he spoke he drove into the gravel sweep of Aimée's front door.

"Will you come in?" Yola asked politely.

He shook his head.

"I have some things to do before we meet this evening," he said, "so make my apologies to Aimée for me."

"I will do that, and thank you again."

Yola smiled at him a little shyly, and without relinquishing the reins he kissed her gloved hand.

"Think of me until then," he said very softly so that he could not be heard by the flunkey waiting to help Yola alight.

His fingers tightened on hers, and despite herself Yola felt a little thrill run through her.

He must have been aware of it, for she saw a sudden glint in his eyes. Then hastily she stepped out of the chaise and went into the house.

Aimée was out, and Yola went up to her bedroom. Taking off the very elegant yellow gown she had worn to tour the Exhibition and the tiny flower-trimmed hat that went with it, she undressed and got into bed.

She told herself that it would be wise to sleep, but instead she found her mind going round and round in circles as she thought of the Marquis.

Last night had been a moment of such exquisite ecstasy that she had to keep telling herself that it might not have meant the same to him.

It was her first kiss, while he had kissed so many women that it could have meant very little to him despite the things he had said.

As he had raised his head and his lips had left hers, she had, because she was shy, hidden her face against his shoulder.

After a moment, as if the silence was more eloquent than words, he had said very quietly:

"You are not disappointed in your first kiss, my darling?"

"I . . . I did not know . . . a kiss could be . . . so wonderful!" Yola whispered.

"I told you that you were like quicksilver in my hands," he said, "and yet for one enchanted moment you have been unable to escape me."

She had given a little laugh of sheer happiness.

Then he put his fingers under her chin and turned her face up to his.

"You are lovely," he said, "unbelievably lovely! And I was right in thinking this was the perfect setting for you."

The moonlight was on her face and her head was silhouetted against the silver water cascading behind her into the pool at their feet.

For a long moment he looked at her, then he was kissing her again with slow, possessive, demanding kisses which made Yola feel as if he made her his and it was impossible to escape from him.

Then as if he knew that anything else they said or did would be mere bathos after they had touched the heights of rapture, he drew her back down the little path which wound between the trees to where the carriage was waiting.

He held her hand closely as they drove back in silence, and only when they reached Aimée's house and the Marquis stepped out to help her alight did he say:

"I will call for you tomorrow morning at ten-thirty and take you to see the International Exhibition."

Yola was so bemused with her own feelings that it was almost hard to understand what he was saying. In fact, she felt as if her voice had died in her throat.

Their eyes met and for one moment they were both very still. Then the Marquis turned away and stepped back into the carriage.

Yola went up the stairs to her bed-room feeling that her heart had turned several somersaults and the whole world was upside down.

Now she told herself she had to be sensible.

Perhaps the ecstasy the Marquis had evoked in her was only because she was so young and so inexperienced.

He had been perceptive enough to realise that she had never been kissed before, but that was not to say that such ignorance was particularly attractive to him—or perhaps it was attractive only as a new experience.

Every moment until she met him again Yola was trying to play down what had happened, to prevent it from having any great significance, or to keep herself from admitting that her previous feelings about the Marquis had completely changed.

And yet the moment she had seen him in Aimée's Salon she had felt as if her whole body became pulsatingly alive and that it was impossible to think of anything except how attractive he looked.

Now as she turned from side to side on the soft pillows, she fought against admitting that she was wildly and crazily in love.

This is what she had always wanted to feel about a man, this is what she knew love would be like, but for the Marquis . . . ?

He was the man she had come to Paris to hate; the man she was certain she despised as a pleasure-seeker; a man whom she suspected of living off money given to him by women; a man whom she had expected to find empty-headed and without any serious side to his nature.

Was she wrong? Or was she merely a stupid, unsophisticated girl who had been swept off her feet by a very experienced and professionally fascinating man?

It was all very difficult to sort out in her brain, and she felt almost as if her own mind had ceased to function, while her body, pulsating with new sensations, had taken over.

It was impossible to consider anything logically or objectively as she had been taught to do.

Instead, she could only feel an irrepressible longing for time to pass quickly before she could see the Marquis again and be with him.

He had said he wanted to talk to her. What did he want to say? What was he going to tell her?

She knew what she wanted to hear, but she told

herself it was asking too much to expect this to be a fairy-tale with an inevitable happy ending.

"I am being very foolish," she told herself a dozen times.

Yet, when it was time to dress for dinner she sprang out of bed with an irrepressible eagerness and knew as she saw her reflection in the mirror that she had never before looked so lovely.

She had deliberately chosen a gown which she had bought from Pierre Floret because it was so pretty, not because it made her look sophisticated as her other gowns did.

Of white crêpe, it was trimmed with real lace, frill upon frill of it forming the fullness of the train behind the swathed front.

Yola thought that in a way it made her appear like a statue of some Greek goddess, and when the Marquis saw her as she entered the Salon he exclaimed:

"You look like Aphrodite rising from the foam!"

She had deliberately not asked Aimée if she could borrow any jewellery, and her only ornamentation was two white roses in her hair and one at her neck, held in place by a narrow ribbon of the same material as her gown.

With her black hair arranged by Felix in a new style, her eyes shining almost blindingly with excitement and happiness, and her lips parted, it would have been impossible for any man not to be moved by her beauty.

The Marquis looked at her, and then without touching her he said:

"I love you! I did not mean to tell you so until later this evening, but it is impossible to find any other words in which to tell you how beautiful you are!"

She moved nearer to him and she wanted him to kiss her as she had never before wanted anything so much.

Instead, he kissed each finger of her hand, then her palm, and finally her wrist.

The feeling of his mouth on her skin made her quiver, and he looked into her eyes to say softly:

"I think the 'Sleeping Beauty' is coming awake."

Yola blushed and the Marquis said:

"Let us go out to dinner. I am taking you to the Café Anglais, but we will not sit in the *Grand Siège* where everyone would admire you. I want you to myself."

There was a possessive note in his voice which thrilled her and she let him lead her across the Hall and help her into the carriage.

Then, when they drove off, she asked, conscious that her voice had deepened a little because she was speaking to him:

"Why do you say I will not be . . . seen in the Café Anglais?"

"Because we are dining in a private room," he answered. "I have ordered our dinner and I thought we deserved a good one after that very unpleasant luncheon."

"But it was such fun!" Yola said.

"I am beginning to find that everything we do together is fun," the Marquis answered, "except when it means a million other things, things I have never known or felt before."

She understood what he was saying and after a moment she replied:

"Everything is very . . . wonderful for me . . . but then that is . . . different because as I have already told you I am only a . . . country mouse and have done none of these . . . things before."

"I am not talking about Exhibitions or sight-seeing," the Marquis said. "I am talking about feelings, Yola, and what you have made me feel is something which I have never felt for anyone else."

"Are you . . . sure of that?"

"Quite, quite sure!" he said positively.

They reached the Café Anglais and he took her up a steep staircase to one of the rooms which was called the *Marivaux*.

It was also known, although the Marquis did not

inform Yola of it, as *le Cabinet des femmes du monde,* because Society women used it when they were frightened of being recognised with their lovers.

It was attractively furnished, and Yola, looking at the elaborately laid table for two, which was decorated with flowers, felt thrilled and flattered because the Marquis wanted to be alone with her.

The waiter opened a bottle of champagne which was already waiting for them in an ice-bucket, and the Marquis took Yola's wrap from her shoulders, put it on a chair, and said:

"I have never seen you in white before."

"Do you . . . like it?"

"I like everything you wear," he answered, "and I am sure the rainbow does not hold a colour that would not become you."

He paused.

"Tonight you look very young, a girl on the threshold of life who has no idea of what lies before her and is thrilled by the sheer excitement of living."

He spoke not in the mocking voice Yola knew so well, but instead in one that was so serious and deep that she looked at him in surprise.

"What are you thinking?" he asked.

"I am asking myself whether you are merely . . . repeating what you have said many times before to many . . . other women, or if your compliments are . . . sincere."

"They are not compliments, Yola," the Marquis said almost angrily, "and I am speaking from my heart."

He walked away from her across the room and stood for a moment looking into a long mirror which was fixed to one wall.

Yola realised he was not staring at his own reflection but looking at her where in her white gown she stood framed against a dark red curtain.

"What have you done to me?" he asked. "I told myself a thousand times today that I am far too old to feel like this."

"How old are you?"

"I am twenty-seven," the Marquis answered, "nearly twenty-eight."

It must be fifteen years, Yola calculated, since he had been at the Castle, unless he had gone to her father's funeral.

Did it mean something important in his life? she wondered.

She had an impulse to confess to him who she was before they became more deeply involved in this strange relationship, but then she told herself that it would be a great mistake to do so.

She had set herself a part to play and she must play it to the end, but she was not certain when the end would come.

They sat down to dinner and she knew that the Marquis was putting himself out to amuse and entertain her.

He told her stories of Paris which made her laugh, described evenings at the Tuileries Palace which could be at times incredibly boring, and spoke of evenings on the Boulevards and at the Dance-Halls, which were a delight.

"There is so much to see and do in Paris," she said, "that I feel if I lived here for twenty years I would only touch the fringe."

"Is that what you want to do?" the Marquis asked. "To live in Paris?"

Yola shook her head.

"It is fascinating for a holiday," she answered, "but I would never really wish to live anywhere but in the country."

She almost held her breath as she waited for his answer.

It came in the shape of a question.

"You do not find it dull?"

Yola shook her head.

"There are horses, gardens, so many things to do . . . I would find it impossible to be bored."

She raised her eyes to his and added:

"Perhaps for a . . . man it could be dull."

"Not if he has money."

It was not the answer Yola had expected and she was tense as the Marquis went on:

"For those who have a big estate there are always things to do, but I have no estate. It was taken from my family in the Revolution."

"And you have not been able to acquire another one?"

"Good land in France is expensive," he replied, "and the sort of house I would like to live in would be more expensive still."

Yola felt some of the happiness she had been feeling ebb away from her as the stream last night had run away from the pool.

She was sure that he was thinking of the Castle and the great Beauharnais estate stretching for miles over the Loire Valley.

He was right, of course. That was the sort of background he should have.

But to obtain it he had to marry a girl he had not seen since she was three; a girl who for all he knew might be hideous or, worse still, as cold and austere as her mother had been.

Yola found herself gripping her fingers together in her lap.

They had finished dinner, a delicious, superlative meal which the Marquis had told her was peculiar to the Café Anglais.

"It is impossible to have better food in the whole of France," the Marquis had said, "and Duglere, the Maître d'Hôtel, tells me that the Czar of Russia, the King of Prussia, and Bismark are to give a banquet here next week, which he is certain will go down in history as the greatest gastronomic feast of the Exhibition Year."

Yola had appreciated every dish, but now that the dinner was finished, she felt as if it had celebrated not the beginning but the end of the dream that had come and gone before it had reached fulfilment.

Quite suddenly she asked herself what she was doing here alone in a private room with a man who was known to be a "lady-killer," a breaker of hearts.

She had heard about him before she came to Paris, and the fact that he was more fascinating and charming than she had anticipated should not have surprised her.

She had merely been foolish to think he should be anything else.

She had embarked upon what *Madame* Renazé had called "a mad escapade," and it had now boomeranged in a manner which she might have guessed it would.

She had fallen in love with the professional heartbreaker and all she would have to show for her adventure was her broken heart.

The table had been cleared except for the flowers, candles, and coffee-cups.

The Marquis put his hand palm-upwards towards Yola.

"What is troubling you?" he asked quietly.

Because she could not resist touching him she put her hand into his.

"Why do you . . . think I am . . . troubled?"

"I told you before, I know everything about you. You are asking yourself why you are here alone with me, and I think too you are a little afraid."

"Afraid?" Yola repeated.

"Yes, afraid," he replied. "You were afraid the first night when you came into the Winter Garden and looked down at the assembled guests, and you were afraid when your eyes met mine."

His fingers tightened on hers as he said:

"Suppose we now dispense with all those secrets and you tell me what you are thinking and feeling, and why you keep that absurd and very unnecessary barrier between us."

"That is not . . . true," Yola tried to say, but she met the Marquis's eyes and the words died away on her lips.

"You are so lovely, my darling," the Marquis said. "So perfect, so unspoilt! If I were wise, I would pick you up in my arms and carry you away to the country, where we would be alone and you would never see anyone but me."

The passion in his voice made Yola instinctively hold a little tighter to his hand.

"I would be very kind to you," the Marquis said softly, "and we would be happy, very, very happy together."

"What are you saying?" Yola enquired.

"I am telling you that I love you," the Marquis replied, "and I think you love me a little."

He smiled as her eyes dropped before his.

"This is the first time you have been in love, my sweet, but let me tell you that you cannot fight against it. It is overwhelming, overpowering, and there is no escape."

"Is . . . is . . . that what you . . . feel?" Yola asked hesitatingly.

"I can tell you truthfully that I am deeply and overwhelmingly in love," the Marquis answered. "And this is also the truth, Yola—it is different from what I have ever felt in the past."

He paused before he went on:

"I have thought myself to be in love a dozen times. I have told myself that it was the real thing, what I had always sought. But some critical part of my mind has always told me that in fact it was not the idealistic love which all men believe waits for them somewhere."

The Marquis's voice was very solemn as he continued:

"I think there is for all of us a voice, like the voices of Joan of Arc, which inspires us to seek perfection, to reach for the superhuman, the Divine."

Yola looked at him in surprise as he went on:

"It is so easy to believe that this cannot and will not happen in ordinary, everyday life. Yet, however much we may deny it, the yearning is there and so is the voice which speaks not in our ears but to what the Church calls our souls."

Yola drew in her breath.

It was so strange that he should be talking of

Joan of Arc, the Saint to whom she had always prayed, the Saint who belonged to the Loire Valley and was a part of her childhood because of the tapestry in the private Chapel at the Castle.

"I see that you understand," the Marquis said with a faint smile. "And that is why, my darling, you will know what I mean when I tell you that now a voice within me says that you are mine as God intended you to be when you were first born."

It seemed impossible that he should be saying such things, and yet, holding tightly to his hand, Yola felt as if every word struck a response within both her heart and her soul.

It was how she had always wanted a man to think and to feel about her, and everything she had ever read and everything she had studied with her father had made her believe that real love was as the Marquis described it.

This was the love she wanted so desperately and believed it would be impossible to find with the man her grandmother and her father had chosen for her as a husband.

"I love . . . you!" she said simply, her eyes shining with a dazzling light.

"My sweet! My darling!" the Marquis said hoarsely, then drew her to her feet and took her in his arms.

He held her closely against him, and as gently as last night his lips sought hers.

He kissed her as if she were something infinitely precious and almost sacred.

Then as he felt the softness of her mouth, the yielding of her body, and the thrills which ran through her, his kiss became more demanding, more intense.

The room where they were ceased to exist and Yola felt as if they were standing in the sunshine on the terrace at home, with the Château behind them and the blossoms in the valley making the whole place a fairy-land of beauty and love.

This was what she had longed for, this was what

she had wanted... Love. The real love which did not count the cost of sacrifice and which demanded nothing but its own perfection.

The Marquis gave a sigh which seemed to relieve some tension within himself. Then he drew Yola onto a sofa which stood at the side of the room, still holding her closely in his arms.

"We have to make plans, my darling," he said, "plans for the future."

"What sort of plans?" Yola murmured.

She felt as if waves of happiness were moving within her so that it was hard to think of anything but the closeness of the Marquis, the touch of his lips and the strength of his arms.

"I cannot have you leave me," the Marquis said. "I want you with me both by day and by night, my precious one."

"That is . . . what I want . . . too."

He kissed her forehead, then her eyes, one after another, and lastly her mouth.

"Tell me again that you love me," he said. "I want to be sure that anything so perfect, so beautiful, is really mine."

"I love you!" Yola said obediently. "I love you so much that it is hard to think of... anything else. I just want to keep repeating that I... love you and hear you say that you . . . love me."

"I adore you! I worship you!"

"Forever?"

He smiled.

"That is what we all ask of life, but where you and I are concerned, my sweet, I believe our love will last forever and a day."

"That is what I want you to . . . say," Yola cried. "Oh, Leo, it is all so... strange and so... exciting, because..."

She was about to say: "Because I am not Yola Lefleur but Marie Teresa de Beauharnais."

Then as she drew in her breath to make the revelation, the Marquis said:

"The reason I took you home early today when we might have spent another few hours together is that I wanted to look at a house I thought would please you."

"A . . . house?" Yola questioned.

"I have found somewhere where we can be together," the Marquis answered. "I am jealous even of the time you spend with Aimée, and if you will agree you can leave tomorrow."

Yola was very still. She felt suddenly as if an icy hand was squeezing her heart, squeezing away her happiness.

"I do not . . . know exactly . . . what you . . . mean."

"It is quite simple," he answered. "I have found an adorable little house standing in its own garden on the very edge of the Bois. I thought you could go there tomorrow."

He smiled and added:

"Then when we have time we will leave Paris and go away somewhere together, somewhere very quiet, my precious, where we can get to know each other."

"Wh-what are you . . . asking me?" Yola faltered.

"I think the right term for it," the Marquis said with a twist of his lips, "is that I am offering you my protection, but what I am really giving you, my sweetheart, is my love, my heart, and everything I possess."

Yola felt as if the room had suddenly gone dark. Then in a voice which hardly seemed to be her own she said:

"Are you . . . asking me to be your . . . mistress?"

"Do you think I would share you with anyone else?" the Marquis asked. "Of course I am asking you to belong to me alone."

He smiled as he went on:

"I cannot deck you, my darling, in jewels such as are worn by La Païva nor can I give you a dozen carriages, each one different to match your gowns, like *Madame* Musard, but I think the love we have for each other will compensate you for many things which unfortunately I cannot afford."

He pulled Yola a little closer to him as he said:

"I believe you when you say you love me, for, *ma belle*, it would be impossible for you to lie to me. That is why I know that while I am not a millionaire and can only keep you in comfort instead of luxury, what is really important is that we will be happy."

He kissed her forehead as he added:

"There is so much I have to teach you, my lovely one. I have awakened my Sleeping Beauty, but she is still not fully aroused, and to make sure that she is will be the most wonderful thing I have ever done in my life."

Yola felt numb.

She told herself that it was just as she should have expected.

Yet somehow it was impossible not to feel shocked and even horrified that all he was prepared to offer her was what he would offer the type of woman whom *Madame* Renazé and Aimée despised.

Because she could not find words to answer him or to explain that what he suggested was impossible, she disentangled herself from his arms and, rising to her feet, said:

"I think . . . I must . . . go home. I have . . . rather a . . . headache."

"We spent too much time at the Exhibition," the Marquis said as he too rose. "But tomorrow after you are rested we will go to see the house I inspected this afternoon. I know it will please you, and when we shut the door behind us we will shut out the world and be alone, you and I, with our love."

Yola did not reply, and for the first time it must have crossed his mind that her response to what he had suggested had not been enthusiastic.

He stood looking at her and after a moment he said:

"What is wrong? Why are you not as pleased as I thought you would be?"

Yola did not reply.

"Why do you say nothing? Why do you look like that?"

He waited for her answer and when it did not come he stepped forward to say:

"You are not playing with me? If you are—if you have lied about your love for me—I think I will kill you!"

He put his arms round her and pulled her roughly against him to turn her face up to his.

"Are you lying?" he asked.

Before she could reply, his mouth was on hers and he was kissing her demandingly, passionately, in a very different way from how he had kissed her before.

She felt the fire on his lips and saw it flare into his eyes.

But because he had taken her by surprise Yola was for the moment only conscious of the hardness of his kiss and that he was hurting her.

Then instinctively she sensed that she had aroused a very different emotion in him from anything she had known before.

She tried to struggle but it was impossible.

His mouth held her captive and he picked her up in his arms and carried her through the curtains which were drawn across one part of the room.

She had not realised before that on the other side was a low couch, and as the Marquis almost threw her down on it Yola gave a little cry.

"You are mine! You cannot escape me!" he said harshly.

He was kissing her again, with angry and almost brutal kisses which burned the softness of her skin.

"No . . . no . . . no . . ." she tried to say.

He kissed her cheeks, her neck, and again her mouth, and she could feel his hands touching her body.

Quite suddenly she was afraid—desperately, terribly afraid of what he might do.

She struggled like an animal in a trap, she twisted her mouth free of his, and as she did so she managed to cry:

"No . . . Leo! No! No! No! You are . . . frightening me! Please . . . Leo . . . please."

It was the cry of a child and it stopped the Marquis as no other plea would have done.

He looked down at her. She saw his expression of suspicion and desire and knew by the way he was breathing that she had aroused, excited, and angered him.

"P-please . . . let me . . . go."

The words were almost strangled in her throat but he heard them and saw the pleading and fear in her face.

Slowly he rose from the couch and hesitatingly Yola raised herself on the cushions against which he had thrown her.

As she did so the Marquis turned and walked back into the part of the room in which they had dined.

There was some champagne left in the bottle that stood in the ice-bucket and he poured himself a glass and drank it off at one gulp.

Yola smoothed down her gown, aware even as she did so that she felt shaken and bruised and that her hands were trembling.

Then, moving very slowly, her eyes dark and apprehensive in her white face, she walked towards the Marquis.

"I will take you home," he said, and he did not look at her.

He crossed the room to pick up her wrap from the chair on which it had been laid.

He opened the door and she preceded him down the stairs.

They waited for a few minutes while the doorman called for the Marquis's carriage, then Yola stepped into it.

Only as they drove away did she say hesitatingly:

"I . . . I am . . . sorry . . . I did not . . . mean to . . . upset you."

"I am sorry too," the Marquis replied. "I forgot how unsophisticated you are."

He smiled as if he mocked himself, before he said:

"Shall we forget what happened tonight and remember only how happy we were beside the cascade in the Bois?"

"Please . . . let us do . . . that."

There was a throb in her voice as if she was not far from tears. The Marquis put his arm round her and drew her very gently against him.

"It is all right, my sweet," he said. "Everything was my fault, and I will not frighten you again."

She put her head against his shoulder but he stared straight ahead as if he was thinking.

After a moment Yola asked:

"You . . . are not . . . angry with . . . me?"

"I am angry with myself," the Marquis answered, "but I am also somewhat bewildered."

Yola waited and after a moment he said:

"There is so much I do not understand. Why are you staying with Aimée, why are you dressed as you are, and what are you expecting to find in Paris?"

Because she knew she could not answer his questions, not at the moment at any rate, Yola turned her face against his shoulder and was very near to tears.

The Marquis held her a little closer.

"You are tired," he said, and his voice was tender. "Go to bed and tomorrow we will talk things over quietly, you and I, and find an answer to everything. I am sure really it is all quite simple."

Yola did not answer and he kissed her hair.

"I love you!" he said. "That is something about which there can be no argument."

It was not a long journey to the Rue du Faubourg Saint-Honoré and as the carriage drove into the courtyard the Marquis said:

"Do not worry about anything, my darling. Tomorrow all the difficulties and problems will seem less worrying and may have vanished completely."

He kissed her hair again and went on:

"I will take you driving, then we will have luncheon somewhere quietly where we can talk. There is a little restaurant at the side of the Seine where you can watch the barges going up and down the river."

"I would . . . like . . . that," Yola managed to say.

"Then that is where we will go," the Marquis said. "Promise me you will go to sleep and not think about anything except our love."

"I . . . I will . . . try."

He took both her hands and kissed them one after another.

"I love you!" he said. "Go to sleep remembering those three words and all they mean. You hold my heart in your hands, my precious one."

The footman opened the door of the carriage, they got out, the Marquis murmured good-night, and Yola went into the house without looking back.

"Has *Madame* returned?" she asked, knowing that Aimée was going out to dinner.

"Yes, *M'mselle, Madame* is alone in the Salon."

Yola ran across the Hall and opened the door.

Aimée must have just come in, because she was standing at the window, pulling off the long black gloves she had worn.

She turned round as Yola entered and gave a little exclamation.

"What has happened?"

Yola walked slowly across the room to sit down on a sofa. She drew a deep breath before she replied:

"The Marquis has . . . asked me to become his . . . mistress!"

Aimée moved to her side.

"And it has upset you?"

She saw the answer in Yola's expression and added:

"My dear child, what else did you expect?"

"I th-thought that he loved me as . . . I love him!"

Aimée sat down beside her.

"You love him?"

"With all my heart!" Yola answered. "He is everything I dreamt of and believed I would find in the man I should marry."

"He *is* the man you will marry," Aimée said softly.

Yola gave a gesture of despair.

"Do you really think I would marry him knowing that he loves me only enough to want me as his mistress?"

Aimée was silent for a moment. Then she said almost sharply:

"Listen to me, Yola."

In response Yola raised her eyes.

"Now listen and try to understand," Aimée said. "The Marquis comes from an aristocratic, noble family and his ancestors served the Kings of France for generations."

She paused before she said clearly and distinctly:

"Marriage for him has nothing to do with love."

"B-but . . . if he . . . loves me . . . ?" Yola faltered.

"He loves you as a woman and I thought when I saw him this morning before he took you to the Exhibition that he was different, and that it was love that had changed him."

"If he . . . really loved me as Yola . . . Lefleur, he would . . . ask me to . . . m-marry him."

"It would be impossible for him to do so," Aimée said positively.

"Why?" Yola enquired.

"Because everything he has been brought up to believe in—everything that is ingrained in him as a part of his blood, of his pride, and of his family—would prevent him from making someone of no consequence and not of equal rank his wife and the mother of his children."

"Then he does not . . . love me!" Yola said. "After all . . . the *Duc* wishes to marry you!"

"That is very different."

"I see no difference."

"Then let me explain," Aimée answered. "The *Duc*

wishes to marry me as his second wife, but I know that however much we mean to each other—and we do mean everything in the world—he would never envisage me in that position unless he already had an heir to the title."

Yola looked surprised and Aimée explained:

"He has three children with his wife. Two of them are boys. She went mad, as sometimes happens, having her third child."

"You are really telling me that the *Duc* would put his family before . . . you?"

"But of course he would!" Aimée said. "It is traditional, built on the unwritten laws that have been followed and obeyed by the French aristocracy for centuries."

Yola was silent, then said in a whisper:

"Do you . . . think the Marquis intends to . . . keep me as his mistress while he goes to the . . . Castle next month to propose . . . marriage to . . . Marie Teresa de Beauharnais?"

Aimée rose to her feet to walk to the mantelpiece.

"This may seem hard for you to understand, Yola," she said, "but I do not think for a moment that the Marquis would consider he was doing anything unusual, reprehensible, or wrong."

"It appals me even to think of it!"

"That is because you are in love and because you have put yourself entirely of your own choice in this impossible situation."

Aimée looked at Yola before she said:

"It is unfair to judge the Marquis when you are deceiving him by disguising yourself as a *demi-mondaine;* a woman who he would never expect for a moment would want marriage or imagine he would suggest it."

"I am shocked!" Yola said defiantly.

"It did not shock your father to take a *chère amie* when he was married to your mother."

"My mother made him desperately unhappy by her behavior," Yola retorted.

"Your father fell in love, and it would have been

understandable, even if he had quite amicable feelings towards your mother, that he should spend some of his time away from home."

"That is the French attitude!"

"And you *are* French, my dear," Aimée replied. "It may seem reprehensible to some other nations, but it is our way of life, whether we or anyone else likes it or not."

"If Leo really loved me as much as he says he does, he would want me as his . . . wife."

"Do you really credit that that would be possible, seeing where he has met you, what you look like, and the attitude of *other* men towards you?"

The way Aimée spoke aroused Yola's attention.

"What do you mean by that?" she enquired.

"I was going to speak to you tonight or tomorrow morning at the very latest," Aimée said, "because, whatever your relationship with the Marquis, you have to leave Paris!"

Chapter Six

Yola stared at Aimée in surprise, and it flashed through her mind that Aimée wished to be rid of her because of the *Duc*.

Then she knew that that was absurd and after a little pause she asked:

"Why must I go?"

Aimée sat down on the sofa and, throwing her gloves onto a table beside her, said:

"The Prince Napoleon has been here."

"What for?" Yola enquired.

"He came to see me," Aimée replied, "because he is determined, completely and absolutely determined, that you should belong to him."

"Then he will be disappointed!" Yola said sharply. "And I am quite prepared to tell him so."

"It is not as easy as that."

"What do you mean?"

"I mean that he can not only harm me, which he has threatened to do, but also the *Duc*, and that is something I cannot allow."

Yola's eyes were wide with astonishment, then she reached to take Aimée's hand in hers.

"You know I would not do anything to hurt either you or the *Duc*, for you both have been so kind to me," she said, "but please explain, because I do not understand."

"The Prince Napoleon is a very important man in Paris," Aimée replied, "and people will do anything rather than incur his enmity. He has a violent temper and like other clever men he can be very spiteful."

"Are you really saying that the Prince expects you to force me into accepting his advances?"

"I mean just that," Aimée replied.

"But it is incredible!"

"Not really," Aimée answered. "He has been very spoilt and in a way he is proud of his reputation with women."

She smiled a little wryly before she went on:

"If you refuse him, he feels, it might make him a laughing-stock that he, who has been the lover of the most fascinating women in Paris, should be turned down by someone of no importance."

"I have never heard anything so ridiculous!" Yola exclaimed.

Aimée smiled again.

"My dear, men are only children, and in Paris they vie with one another in showing off their amatory conquests just as Englishmen value their prowess in the hunting-field or on the race-course."

"How could he hurt you?" Yola asked, curious.

"The Prince, like his sister, Princess Matilde, mixes with the intelligent and artistic set in Paris. If he really declared me to be his avowed enemy, the majority of people who grace my Salon would be too afraid to accept my invitations."

"And the *Duc*?" Yola asked.

"That is something far more serious," Aimée replied, and her voice was soft as it always was when she spoke of the man she loved.

"But the *Duc* is so important," Yola said. "He is a man of such distinction that it is hard to imagine that anyone would listen to what the Prince said about him."

"The *Duc*, although he belongs to one of the most ancient families in France, has accepted the new Emperor, which many other noblemen have not done," Aimée explained. "He is therefore *persona grata* at the Tuileries, but at the same time he has many interests which concern the Prince."

"What sort of interests?"

"Some of them concern the development of the Arts, while others are plans to restore prosperity to the parts of France which at the present are not of any interest to the Emperor."

"That is certainly important," Yola agreed.

"It is important to France and important to the *Duc* himself," Aimée said. "He has spent so much of his time, his thoughts, and his own money on these projects that I could not bear for him now to have them taken from him and to be left outside the negotiations that are taking place."

"No, of course not. I understand," Yola said. "But even if I leave Paris, will the Prince not try to get in touch with me?"

"I have thought of that," Aimée replied, "and I shall tell him that you have made up your mind to return to a very obscure part of France where you will be married."

She pressed Yola's hand as she said:

"That you are to be married is certainly true, at least I hope so."

Yola did not reply to this, she merely kissed Aimée and said:

"I shall always be grateful for your kindness to me. I will leave early tomorrow morning before there is any possibility of His Imperial Highness calling to see me."

She went up to her room and told the maid who was waiting to attend to her to bring in her trunks.

It took them two hours to pack the beautiful gowns that Yola had purchased from Pierre Floret and there were so many of them that she had to borrow two of Aimée's trunks.

When finally everything was finished and she could get into bed, her problems kept her tossing restlessly in the darkness.

She told herself she must think of what had happened calmly and logically as her father would have wished her to do.

But while her brain told her one thing, her whole

body cried out that the love that the Marquis professed for her should be great enough for him to offer her marriage.

Whatever Aimée might say, whatever she knew about the traditional French *mariage de convenance,* she wanted a Cinderalla story for herself.

She wished to be loved without having anything to offer a man in return except her heart.

She wanted the Marquis to want her as she wanted him, just as a person, without her Castle, without her fortune, even without knowing that her breeding was as good as his.

Her logical mind told her that this was quite impossible and that Aimée was right: the Marquis was French and Frenchmen did not think like that.

But something child-like and idealistic made Yola feel that she could not compromise, could not accept that the Marquis should love her as a man but not as an aristocrat.

At times she wanted to cry, remembering that for one moment when he told her of his love she had touched the heights of ecstasy and happiness, only to find it dashed away and to know that it, like a will-o'-the-wisp, was now out of reach.

"If I marry him in the circumstances," she told herself, "I would never again believe his protestations of love. I would never think that he felt as I did or that our love was Divine."

She clenched her fingers together in the darkness as she whispered:

"He would have the woman he loved as his mistress and the Castle as well, while I would have only a man who did not love me enough to offer a wedding-ring."

When dawn came she rose to pull back the curtains and look out the window onto the garden.

In the distance she could see the grey roofs of Paris and the sky grey and a little overcast above them.

It seemed to Yola an omen of what her life would be in the future: a life without the sunshine of love which had transformed her in such a way that she could never again return to what she had been before.

"How could this have happened?" she asked. "and why should I have to suffer?"

She knew the answers only too well. It was her own fault. She had done an outrageous thing by coming to Paris.

She had behaved as no other lady in her position would have done, and now she was being punished for it—punished so that the rest of her life would be as grey as the sky and love would always elude her.

It was in that moment that she decided she would not marry the Marquis.

She could not imagine a more agonising hell on earth than to love him so overwhelmingly and to know that what he offered her in return was not the real love of a man for a woman who belonged to him so that nothing else mattered.

"I can never forget! I can never forgive!" she said aloud.

Although it was still very early, she did not pull back the curtains but lay watching the light creep across the sky, thinking that at home it would be touching the turrets on the Castle and making them glow as if they were burnished with gold.

It occurred to her in that moment that the Castle lay at the root of all her troubles.

It was so beautiful, so alluring, that she was certain the real reason the Marquis would not give her his name as well as his heart was that in doing so he supposed he would be forced to relinquish it.

"I will write him a letter telling him that I will not see him again," Yola told herself.

Then she remembered that she would have to persuade her grandmother to cancel his invitation to the Castle.

For a moment she felt almost sick at the thought of the row that would ensue, of the anger her grandmother would feel at having to change her plans.

Worst of all would be the difficulty of trying to

explain why she had suddenly decided not to marry the Marquis and that she did not wish him to come to Beauharnais.

'I will not write,' Yola thought. 'I will tell Aimée to tell him the same story she will tell the Prince Napoleon.'

That, she thought, would dispose of Yola Lefleur, and somehow when she was back at home she would think of some excuse why the Marquis should not come courting Marie Teresa de Beauharnais.

The maid called her and she rose and dressed herself in a new and elegant silk gown which had a light cape she could wear over it for travelling.

Its colour was emerald green and it made her skin look very white and her eyes almost the colour of emeralds.

There was a smart little hat trimmed with ivy leaves to match and Yola was just about to put it on her head when there was a knock at the door.

The maid went to open it and she heard a footman say:

"*Monsieur le Marquis* de Montereau has called to see *M'mselle!*"

Yola looked at the clock on the mantelshelf. It was not yet nine o'clock and she knew that Aimée would not yet be awake, for she invariably slept late.

Her first impulse was to tell the Marquis she would not see him. Then she felt he must have a reason for calling so early and he might insist, which would make a scene in front of the servants.

She put her hat down on the dressing-table and said to the maid:

"Inform *Monsieur le Marquis* that I will be down in a few minutes."

The maid gave the message to the footman and when the door was shut Yola said:

"I do not wish *Monsieur* to realise I am leaving, but order a carriage to be ready for me in half an hour's time. There is a train at just after ten o'clock which I intend to catch."

"Very good, *M'mselle,*" the maid replied. "I will

see to everything, and no-one shall know that you are packed or departing until *Monsieur le Marquis* has left."

"Thank you," Yola said.

She glanced at her reflection in the mirror and saw that after a sleepless night her face was very white and there were lines under her eyes.

Because she was returning home she had not used any mascara on her eye-lashes, rouge on her cheeks, or even salve on her lips.

She wondered if the Marquis might think she looked strange and different from the way she had before. Then she told herself that it was not of the least consequence and after today she would never see him again.

She was determined to be calm and not let him know what she was feeling.

Yet as she walked down the stairs her heart was thumping violently in her breast and her fingers were cold.

The Marquis was waiting for her in the Salon, standing at one of the long windows looking out onto the garden. As she entered, he turned and she saw that he too was pale and his face was lined as if he also had spent a sleepless night.

"You . . . wish to see . . . me?" Yola asked, and her voice sounded strange even to herself.

"It is early," the Marquis answered, "but I could not wait and somehow I felt you would be awake."

Feeling as if her feet would hardly carry her, Yola crossed the room to sit down on a chair which had its back to the window, hoping that the Marquis would not be able to read in her eyes what she was feeling.

As it happened, he did not look at her but walked to stand a little way from her with his back to the empty fireplace.

"I have been walking about all night," he said.

"Walking?" Yola questioned in surprise.

"I wanted to think. God knows where I went, but

I stood for a long time beside the Seine, seeing your face in the water."

"I . . . I do not . . . understand."

"I know that," the Marquis answered. "And I know, as I have always known, what you were thinking last night and what you felt."

She did not speak but she clasped her fingers together in her lap.

"That is why I want to give you an explanation," the Marquis went on, "to try to make you understand why I behaved as I did."

There was a note in his voice that Yola did not recognise and she glanced at him and then looked away again.

"We have told each other very little about ourselves," the Marquis said. "There has never seemed to be time for it. But I think you know that my grandfather was guillotined in the Revolution and all our estates were confiscated."

He spoke the words casually, as if it was not of any great importance, and continued:

"My father was therefore very poor and when he died he was able to leave my mother only a mere pittance. But through the great kindness of a distant cousin, the *Comte* de Beauharnais, I was well and expensively educated."

Yola drew in her breath but did not speak, and the Marquis went on:

"What is more, the *Comte* took us to live in his Castle in the Loire Valley."

He paused before he continued in a low voice:

"I cannot tell you how happy I was there. There were not only horses to ride and a thousand things to do which would delight any small boy, but there was also the Castle itself."

He paused before he said:

"It is without exception the most beautiful, perfect place I have ever seen in my life. As a child it was not only the embodiment of all my dreams, but it inspired me in a way which is hard to understand."

Yola did understand. It was the effect the Castle always had on people; it was the effect it had on her.

"Then when I was nine," the Marquis continued, "the *Comte* died and his son succeeded him; a man to whom I gave a kind of hero-worship; a man who was the best and most wonderful friend anyone could have."

Yola felt the tears come into her eyes at this tribute to her father and she looked down at her hands in case the Marquis should see the expression on her face.

"The new *Comte* de Beauharnais not only carried on my education, which his father had begun," he went on, "but he taught me many things himself and his intelligence and his wisdom were something I shall never forget."

He sighed.

"Unfortunately, his wife was very different from him."

Yola longed to agree: "Very different!" remembering only too well what her mother had been like.

"The *Comtesse* was a religious fanatic," the Marquis continued, "and she managed to make life at the Castle unbearable not only for her husband but also for the many relations who lived there."

He made a gesture with his hand as he said:

"One by one they left, and finally, because she was so unpleasant to my mother, we left too."

"Where did you . . . go?" Yola asked, feeling that because he had paused some comment was expected from her.

"The *Comte* bought us a house on the outskirts of Paris," the Marquis replied. "He sent me to the best and finest school in France, and engaged tutors for me in the holidays, with whom I travelled to various parts of the world, including Italy, Greece, and England. He planned everything as if I were his—son."

Yola was suddenly still. She was beginning to understand.

"And that was what he intended me to be," the Marquis said, "and what he explained to me quite simply when I was eighteen."

Yola felt the Marquis must hear the beating of her heart as he went on:

"The *Comte* had one child, a daughter. She was three years old when I last saw her. He told me it was the dearest wish of his life—and that was why he had educated me so generously—that I should marry Marie Teresa and become the owner of Beauharnais Castle."

The Marquis was silent and after a moment Yola managed to say:

"The idea . . . pleased you?"

"I was at first stunned," the Marquis replied. "Then I knew that it was a gift so stupendous, so fantastic, that I could hardly believe the truth of it."

"Did you . . . suggest that you might . . . see the . . . girl you were to . . . marry?"

"Naturally I suggested it, but the *Comte* replied that he thought it would be a mistake."

" 'My daughter is going, I believe, to be a great beauty,' he told me, 'but colts are often ungainly before they grow to their full capabilities and I want you to see Marie Teresa at her best.'

"He smiled and added: 'There is plenty of time.' "

The Marquis walked a few steps away from the mantelshelf and back again.

"The *Comte* repeated the same thing some years later when I asked him again if I could meet his daughter.

" 'There is no hurry, my dear Leo,' he said. 'I want you to meet Marie Teresa when she is old enough to fall in love with you and you with her.'

"He laughed and added: 'You must allow me to stage-manage this romance in my own way, and no Producer ever had a more attractive hero or heroine!'

" 'Or a better stage set!' I added.

"The *Comte* laughed.

" 'I thought you would think that. The Castle was made for love, which is something it has not had since I have lived there. You will change that, Leo, you and Marie Teresa.' "

The Marquis's voice died away, then he said:

"It was after this last conversation, when I was twenty-three, that I came to an important decision."

"What was . . . that?" Yola asked.

"I knew that I could not marry a wife who was not only wealthy but possessed the Castle of my dreams unless I too had something to offer. I therefore determined to make myself into a rich man."

"A . . . rich man?" Yola echoed in surprise.

"I realised it was not going to be easy," the Marquis said, "because in fact I had nothing but a very generous allowance which the *Comte* made me. However, I thought about it very seriously and told him what I intended to do. He gave me his blessing although I fancy he was slightly skeptical."

"What did you intend to do?"

"I realised that impoverished noblemen were to be found by the dozens in Paris," the Marquis answered, "and they were often an embarrassment to the Emperor and a large number of other members of the very rich, luxurious, extravagant society there."

He spoke as if he was thinking again of the decision he had made and how hard it had been.

"I also have a constitutional dislike of asking for help," he added sharply.

"So what . . . did you do?"

"I introduced myself to Paris as a rich, carefree young man."

"Rich?" Yola queried in astonishment.

"I borrowed a certain sum of money from a friend," the Marquis said, "not the *Comte*, as I had had so much from him already. I promised to repay it in two years and I swore to myself that I would not fail him or myself."

"But how could you repay the money?"

The Marquis smiled mockingly.

"Men are nearly as susceptible as women to flattery, not about their looks but about their possessions. Paris was filled with men vying with one another to show off their wealth, which they expended in a profligate manner on women who spent it as fast as they could make it."

"I do not . . . understand how that could . . . affect you," Yola said.

At the same time, because he had spoken of "women" she felt a little stab of jealousy.

"I made myself amusing and useful to the men who were to be found at every important party, every distinguished dinner. Sometimes, when they found me accommodating in repeating what I had heard passing from one Financier to another, they showed me where there was money to be made."

"On the Bourse?"

"On the Bourse, on the race-course, on the money-changes. There is always someone 'in the know,' always a man who is a little more intelligent and a little brighter than those round him."

"And you made money in . . . such a way?"

"I made money because no-one realised how much I needed it," the Marquis answered.

He gave a little laugh.

"I am not a millionaire, but when two weeks ago I received a letter from Beauharnais, I told myself that I will not go there empty-handed."

"A letter?" Yola questioned, knowing only too well to what he referred.

"It was a letter from the Dowager *Comtesse*, the wife of the *Comte* who had originally befriended my mother and me," the Marquis explained. "She invited me to the Castle next month because Marie Teresa is at last eighteen and grown up."

"You knew . . . why you had been . . . asked?" Yola enquired.

"I knew I had to fulfill my promise to the *Comte*, marry Marie Teresa, and run the Castle and the estates as he had wished."

Yola drew in her breath but it was impossible to speak.

"Everything was plain sailing, everything that had been planned for me since I was nine years old had now come to fruition," the Marquis said, "and then—I met you!"

He looked at Yola before he said:

"Last night I asked the river why in God's name you had to come into my life just at this moment—then I knew the answer."

"Wh-what was . . . it?"

Yola could hardly breathe the words.

"It was fate—fate that we should meet—fate that I should fall in love—fate that I should learn that love is greater than possessions, greater even than the Castle I had longed for all my life."

It seemed to Yola as if she could not be hearing him aright.

She looked up at him, saw the expression in his eyes, and felt that her heart stopped beating.

"That is why, my precious darling," the Marquis said very quietly, "I have come here so early in the morning to ask you if you will be my wife!"

Time seemed to stand still.

Then the Marquis saw the colour come into Yola's pale cheeks and a light into her eyes that made her suddenly radiant. It was like the sun coming up over the horizon to sweep away the night.

She looked at him incredulously as if she could not believe what she had heard, and yet her whole body seemed to have come alive.

"D-do you . . . mean . . . that?"

"I mean it!" the Marquis answered. "But because I feel I am betraying the man who did more for me than any other human being could do for another, because I am at the moment honour-bound to a girl I have not seen since she was a baby, I am going to Beauharnais today to explain my position before we can be married."

"Going . . . to . . . Beauharnais?" Yola repeated almost stupidly.

It was difficult to think, difficult to be conscious of anything but the rapture springing within her.

He loved her! He loved her!

She felt as if she had wings to fly and the whole room was lit with a golden light that enveloped them both.

"I have already sent a telegraph to announce my arrival," the Marquis said. "I shall return tomorrow, and then, my little love, you shall tell me about yourself."

He looked down at her. Although he did not move she felt as though he took her in his arms and his lips were on hers.

"I love you!" he said very quietly. "I love you as I did not know it was possible to love anyone!"

"Oh . . . Leo . . ."

The words which came from Yola's lips were only a sigh. Her eyes met his.

"If you look at me like that," the Marquis said in a low voice, "I shall not be able to leave you. You must not tempt me, my precious, or I shall break my promise to myself to do what has to be done in a decent and honourable manner."

"I . . . understand."

"I knew you would."

With an almost superhuman effort he turned and walked away from her towards the door.

Only as he reached it did Yola manage to ask:

"At what . . . time are you . . . leaving Paris?"

"I believe there is a train about midday," he answered. "But I cannot stay with you, my darling, until then, and you know the reason why."

His eyes were on her lips and she felt as if he kissed them.

Then before she could speak, before she could hardly realise what was happening, he had gone and she heard the sound of his chaise driving away from the front door.

With a little cry she ran up the stairs and without even knocking burst into Aimée's bed-room.

The maid was already there, pulling back the curtains, and as Yola stood beside the bed, Aimée looked up at her with sleepy eyes.

"What is it?"

"I have won! Oh, Aimée, I have won!" Yola cried. "Leo has been here. He has asked me to marry him!"

Aimée sat up in bed.

"He has asked you to marry him? Yola, how wonderful!"

"I had decided I should go home and never see him again, but now everything has changed . . . everything will be perfect!"

"I am so happy for you," Aimée said, but there was just a hint of wistfulness in her voice.

Yola put her arms round her and kissed her.

"Everything will come right for you too," she said. "I am sure of it. Thank you . . . thank you for all your kindness!"

She kissed Aimée again and added hastily:

"I must leave. I have to be at Beauharnais before he arrives there."

"Then hurry!" Aimée smiled. "And do not forget to invite me to your wedding."

"I will not forget," Yola replied, and ran from the room.

* * *

As the train carried her away from Paris and out into the countryside, which was bright with blossoms, Yola thanked God for having answered her prayers.

She thought that her father must know and be pleased that everything he had planned was taking place just as he would have wished it.

"I am so happy, Papa!" Yola said. "But how could I have ever guessed the reason why Leo was at every party, why his name was always in the newspapers, and why everybody gossipped about him?"

She was intelligent enough to understand exactly the kind of aura the Marquis had created for himself.

She was quite sure he was right in knowing that the rich are interested only in the rich, that people want to give only to those who have, never to those who have not.

It was a clever plan but could not have been carried out unless the Marquis himself was extremely intelligent, witty, and charming in a manner which made him sought after not only by men but also by women.

It was impossible for Yola not to feel a little pang of jealousy when she thought of how many women must have loved him.

Then she told herself that no woman could have a greater tribute laid at her feet than that the Marquis should ask her to be his wife, knowing nothing about her, believing her to be of no importance socially and with the stigma of moving in the company of *demi-mondaines*.

"He loves me! He really loves me!" she told herself over and over again to the accompaniment of the wheels.

Aimée's servants had reserved a whole carriage for her on the train, but even so she knew that her grandmother would be horrified if she learnt she had travelled alone.

But for the moment nothing mattered. Her grandmother was always horrified over small trifles, but it was nothing to what she would have felt, Yola thought, if she had gone home, as she had intended, to say that she would not marry the Marquis.

Now no-one would know what she had done or the outrageous step she had taken in going to Paris to stay with Aimée Aubigny.

No-one would know except—the Marquis!

It was almost as if a voice in the carriage spoke the words aloud.

For a moment Yola was startled.

Then it suddenly struck her that he might be angry. After all, no man liked being deceived, no man would want to be made a fool of, and that in fact was what she had done to him.

'It is not true, I did not mean it like that!' Yola cried silently to herself.

Yet she was acutely aware that the Marquis might not be so rapturously happy as she expected when he arrived at the Castle and found that Marie Teresa de Beauharnais was in fact Yola Lefleur!

'He will understand,' Yola reassured herself.

Then she knew that shadowing her radiant happiness there was a small cloud of fear.

It was not menacing, it did not encroach upon her in the way she had felt when she was told she had to marry the Marquis, but nevertheless it was there.

A small patch in the midst of so much light, and she felt as she neared Langeais as if it grew and turned into a stern and accusing expression in the Marquis's eyes.

The way he had looked at her this morning and the things he had said made her feel as if he carried her up into the heart of the sun itself.

But now she was afraid, even while she told herself she was being unnecessarily apprehensive.

The train reached Langeais, and as Yola in her agitation to leave Paris had forgotten to telegraph her grandmother that she would be arriving, there was of course no carriage to meet her at the station.

She was, however, known to the Station Master, and after she had explained that she had left hurriedly and had had no time to notify the Castle, a hackney-carriage was obtained for her.

Her luggage was put into the Station Master's office to be kept safe until it could be collected by the Castle servants.

The promise of rain that had overcast the sky in Paris had not materialised, and now there was sunshine, which Yola told herself was a sign of good luck.

'Everything will be all right,' she thought, and hugged to herself the idea that he loved her, loved her enough to sacrifice everything, even the Castle.

She thought again of the warm way in which the Marquis had spoken of her father, and now looking back she remembered various things that might have given her an idea of what her father was planning for her in the future.

She had always known that he had longed for a son to inherit, and that it would have been against his every instinct to leave her unprotected, at the mercy of fortune-hunters.

'Papa loved me,' Yola thought, 'and he also loved Leo.'

She could imagine how he had planned that he would be instrumental in bringing them together.

She had been sure that once the period of mourning for her mother was over, the Castle would be filled with the relations and friends who had been excluded from it for so long.

Then, in the right atmosphere, that would have been the moment when her father would have asked Leo to come and stay so that they should meet.

"That is what you would have done, Papa," Yola said to him now in her heart. "But perhaps this way it is even more exciting, because we might so easily never have realised how great our love is for each other."

The carriage crossed the Loire and then the Indre and now they were driving through fields filled with spring flowers towards the orchards covered in blossoms.

Then the Castle was in sight.

The sunshine was on it and its towers and turrets were silhouetted against the green forest behind it.

The white stone with which it was built glowed with a light that made it seem almost to float above its terraces.

It was so beautiful, so fairy-like, that Yola felt tears come into her eyes as she remembered how the Marquis had said she was like the Sleeping Beauty.

Now she was awake—awake to realise that her father had been right when he had said this was a Castle made for love.

'I will make Leo happy and we will have many children,' Yola thought, 'so that the Castle will never seem cold, austere, and empty as it did when I was a child.'

The horse clop-clopping along the dusty road carried her nearer still and she thought that the Castle now looked as if it might fly away in the sunlit sky and be nothing but a mirage.

Then she told herself she had nothing to fear.

It was real, it was there, and she would be waiting for Leo when he arrived and he would understand.

There was still, however, just a tiny tremor of fear in Yola's breast as the carriage drove through the gold-tipped wrought-iron gates and up the steep incline to the court-yard.

As it drew to a standstill the servants came hurrying through the front door, the old Butler with an expression of surprise on his face.

"We were not expecting you, *M'mselle,*" he said reproachfully.

"I know," Yola smiled, "but I had to leave Paris earlier than I expected."

She was thinking of a plausible excuse to explain her precipitate return to her grandmother, and found one before she reached the Salon.

"Yola! My dear child!" the *Comtesse* exclaimed. "Why did you not let me know you were coming?"

"It was all very unexpected, *Grandmère,*" Yola replied. "One of the members of the household was taken ill and as it would have been inconvenient for them to have me there any longer, I left."

"Quite right, *ma chérie,*" the *Comtesse* approved. "At the same time, I cannot bear to think that there was not a carriage at the station to meet you. I suppose the maid who accompanied you has waited to take the next train back."

Yola did not answer because she had no wish to lie any further, and her grandmother, not noticing her silence, said:

"As it happens, I am delighted that you are here. In fact I was just about to telegraph to you to return."

"You were, *Grandmère*? But why?" Yola asked.

"I have had a telegram from the Marquis," her grandmother explained, "asking if he might arrive this evening."

Yola forced herself to look surprised, and her grandmother said:

"I cannot imagine why he wishes to come a fortnight earlier than he was expected, but even if I had had the chance to refuse I would not have done so."

"No, of course not, *Grandmère*," Yola agreed. "But we have no time in which to invite a party to meet him."

She was trying only to speak naturally and to behave as her grandmother expected, but she knew that she wanted nobody else there; she wanted to meet Leo alone.

She went to the window and thought of the pleasure it would give her to show him round the Castle where he had lived as a little boy and to see if he noticed any of the improvements which she and her father had made.

There had not been a great deal that she and her father could do, as it had always involved an argument or a quarrel with her mother.

But they had put on show a great many of the treasures which had not been very well displayed in her grandmother's time, and Yola thought they made the inside of the Castle look even more beautiful than it had before.

Now she told herself excitedly that there were so many more things she wanted to do, with which Leo could help and advise her.

All the rooms that had been closed in her mother's time would be opened and the bed-rooms would be redecorated, and they would place new curtains in the Dining-Hall.

It would all be exciting because he would be beside her, because she knew that they had the same taste and that their minds, like their hearts, were linked together.

"You are not listening to me, Marie Teresa!" she heard her grandmother say behind her.

"I am sorry, *Grandmère.* My thoughts were far away. What did you say?"

"I asked if you would see the Chef and order a dinner which you think the Marquis would appreciate. I made some suggestions this morning, but I am sure you know better than I do what young people like."

Yola was not deceived. She knew quite well that her grandmother was longing to say at dinner, if the Marquis enjoyed it, that the menu had been Yola's choice.

It was another way of showing her off to the Marquis, and she thought how angry it would have made her a week ago! But now it was something she wanted to do, something she could do for him, and she said eagerly:

"Of course, *Grandmère,* I will go to see the Chef now, but I am sure your choice has been an excellent one."

"I would rather it was yours, *ma chérie,*" her grandmother replied.

"I suppose there will be four of us for dinner, if your friend is still with you."

"When I learnt the Marquis was coming, I suggested that she should return to Tours."

"Surely that was very high-handed, *Grandmère?*"

"To tell the truth, my dear, I found her rather a bore," her grandmother answered.

Yola knew that the real reason why her grandmother had sent her friend away was because she had no intention of allowing the Marquis to be distracted from anything but the girl he was to marry.

It struck Yola that perhaps her grandmother was feeling as nervous as Yola herself was, but in a different way.

The Marquis was a mature man, and he might, after all these years, have very different ideas about whom he would marry.

Then she thought with a little smile that her

grandmother was supremely confident that no-one who was not a lunatic would refuse the Castle and the Beauharnais estates.

She went from the Salon, her heart singing with happiness, and ran upstairs to her bed-room.

It was a very beautiful room, which her father had decorated for her, and the colours, the furniture, and the pictures were all treasures they had enjoyed together.

She knew that once she was married she would move into the Master Suite, which had always been occupied alone by her father because her mother preferred the austerity of the single bed-room that was almost like a nun's cell.

In the Master Suite, which stood at one of the corners of the Castle, there was a view over the valley that was unsurpassed by any other Castle Yola had ever visited.

There, one could see not only the Indre moving silver through the valley but catch a distant glimpse of the Loire, wide and majestic, carrying the life-giving water which made "the Garden of France" the most beautiful and fertile place in the whole country.

'We will look at it together,' Yola thought, and suddenly felt breathless with excitement and anticipation.

She ran down to the kitchen, changed a few of the dishes on the menu, and ordered the most superb wines in her father's cellar.

Then she went out to the garden to pick some flowers for the Marquis's bed-room.

The garden was full of flowers which were grown for the house and arranged with an artistry which her father had insisted was part of the beauty of the Castle itself.

Yola wanted to put something personal in the Marquis's room and she found a rose bush almost in bloom and thought it would remind him of the buds she had worn in her hair the night he had kissed her in the Bois.

She arranged them in a little blue Sèvres vase and put them beside his bed, then she chose her favourite books and put them there too.

'I love him! I love him!' she thought, looking round to see if there was anything else she could do.

Then, after talking to her grandmother for a little while, she went back upstairs to decide what she should wear.

The noon train from Paris reached Langeais at about five-thirty in the afternoon, which meant that the Marquis would arrive at the Castle at six o'clock.

Yola decided to wear an afternoon-gown in which to receive him. Then, if they had dinner a little later than usual, she would have time to change into something very glamorous in which to celebrate their first meal together in the Castle.

Her luggage had arrived and while the maids were busy unpacking it she chose to put on a gown that was very simple and made her look very young.

She thought it was one of *Monsieur* Floret's masterpieces as a summer-dress.

It was fashioned of broderie anglaise threaded through with turquoise-blue ribbons, and there was a huge bow of the same colour at the back of the gown, giving it almost the effect of a bustle.

Yola showed one of the maids how to arrange her hair in the style which Felix had created for her. Then, wearing no jewellery, she went down to wait in the Salon with her grandmother.

"That is another very unusual gown, *ma chérie,*" the *Comtesse* exclaimed as Yola entered the room. "I thought the one in which you arrived was rather extraordinary but I did not like to say anything. Can that possibly be the latest fashion?"

"It is indeed, *Grandmère.* The small crinoline is finished. There is to be no hoop, no whale-bones to make one uncomfortable."

"I suppose it is becoming," her grandmother said. "At the same time, it looks a little strange to my eyes. I wonder what the Marquis will think."

"Of course he will have to 'get his eyes to,' like everyone else," Yola replied. "You know a fashion always looks peculiar the first time one sees it."

"Yes, that is true," the *Comtesse* agreed. "I remember that when I first saw the crinoline I was astonished, but I must say I am glad they are finished. They took up far too much room in the carriage."

"And were very immodest if one bent over," Yola added, laughing.

"I agree," the *Comtesse* replied. "And at least with this new vogue a lady will not show her ankles."

"No, *Grandmère*," Yola agreed demurely.

Hardly listening to what was being said, she was waiting for the sound of the horses' hoofs and the wheels of the carriage outside in the court-yard.

One window of the Salon looked out onto the front of the Castle and she moved towards it as if she could not restrain herself from watching for the Marquis's arrival.

"If he sees you peering out at him," her grandmother's voice said behind her, "he will think it inquisitive and perhaps uncontrolled. I know you are curious, Marie Teresa, but remember, it is part of our breeding not to show emotions, whatever they may be."

Yola wondered what her grandmother would think if she knew how emotional the Marquis had been in expressing his love for her.

She also knew that her grandmother's rebuke was a very mild one because she was so delighted that the opposition and arguments Yola had put forward at first, at the idea of the Marquis visiting the Castle, had now apparently been forgotten.

It was then that Yola heard the carriage arrive and felt herself tremble.

What would he say? What would he think when he saw her?

Because she was so nervous she instinctively went to stand by her grandmother's chair and knew as she did so that the old lady was also tense.

It seemed to be a very long wait, although it was only a few moments before she heard footsteps coming up the wide staircase.

They were moving slowly because the Butler was getting on in years and it was impossible for him to hurry.

The door of the Salon opened.

"*Monsieur le Marquis* de Montereau, *Madame!*" the Butler announced.

Yola drew in her breath and held on to the back of her grandmother's chair until her knuckles were white.

He came into the room and she thought he looked more attractive and more arresting than she had ever seen him.

He was not dwarfed by the Castle, but seemed to fit into it as if he was already a part of the great edifice.

He crossed the room with a grace that was peculiarly his own and taking her grandmother's hand raised it to his lips.

"I am delighted to see you again, Leonide," the *Comtesse* said, smiling. "Forgive me if I do not get up, but my knees are a little tiresome these days."

"I cannot tell you what a pleasure it is to be here again, *Madame*, and I have never forgotten your kindness to me when I was a boy."

"You were a very nice little boy," the *Comtesse* said, "and I will not be banal and say how you have grown!"

The Marquis laughed an easy, natural laugh.

"And now," the *Comtesse* said, "I shall present you to someone else who has grown. I can hardly believe that after all these years you will remember my granddaughter, Marie Teresa."

Yola curtseyed and because she was shy as well as excited she could not look at the Marquis.

Her eye-lashes were dark against her pale cheeks, then as she heard him say: "I am delighted to meet you, Marie Teresa!" she rose and looked directly into his eyes.

Then as she did so she felt as if she had been struck by a streak of lightning; for incredibly, unbelievably, there was not even a glint of recognition in his eyes!

Chapter Seven

Standing in her own bed-room, Yola felt as if she had encountered a hurricane and was unable to think and hardly able to breathe.

They had not been long in the Salon before her grandmother suggested they go upstairs to dress for dinner.

But the Marquis had talked easily, amusingly, and in a manner which did not seem to be in the least assumed, and yet his behaviour towards her was that of an absolute stranger.

She could not believe, could not credit, that any man could act so well.

As she listened to him speaking to her grandmother of the old days, saying how glad he was to be back again, it was hard to think that this was the same man who had said that he loved her and would sacrifice everything and anything because of his love.

It was impossible for him not to have recognised her, and she asked only for one glance from his eyes, one smile from his lips, to reassure her, to tell her that he understood and forgave her deception.

But it also seemed unbelievable that he had not been startled at seeing her when he entered the Salon, and that he was able to look straight at her and talk to her with just the ordinary courtesy of a visitor.

'Perhaps I shall be able to have a word with him

alone before dinner,' Yola thought, and hurriedly began to undress for her bath.

It was, however, very hard to decide what she should wear.

She had intended to put on the dress that she had worn the night when they had first dined together and he had kissed her in the Bois.

Now she changed her mind. Instead, she let the maid dress her in a gown she had never worn before, but because it was the soft pink of a rose, it made her think of the roses in the garden.

It might make the Marquis remember that they were in "the Garden of France" and more especially that roses were the flowers of love.

Yola hurried, but even so she delayed so long trying to make herself look her best, worrying over the arrangement of her hair and choosing which jewellery she was to wear, that when finally she went down to the Salon it was to find that the Marquis and her grandmother were there before her.

"I was hoping that some of the old servants whom I knew as a boy would still be here," the Marquis was saying. "Dubac, for instance, who taught me to ride, must, I imagine, have retired."

"He is dead," the *Comtesse* replied, "but you will recall Albert, who has taken his place?"

"Yes, of course!" the Marquis exclaimed. "I remember Albert well, and old Cargris, the gardener —is he still alive?"

"He has retired," the *Comtesse* said, "but I know it would give him great pleasure if you would call and see him in his cottage near the gates."

"I certainly will do that," the Marquis said.

Dinner was announced and he gave his arm to the *Comtesse*, and Yola following behind them felt ignored and unnoticed.

How could he possibly behave in such a manner to her if he still loved her?

A thought struck her like a blow: suppose he was so angry at her deception that she had lost his love forever?

She looked at him apprehensively across the flower-decorated table.

Although it was still light outside, the curtains had been drawn and the huge silver candelabrum which had never been used in her mother's time had been brought from the safe to light the table.

As she studied the Marquis while he talked to her grandmother she thought he looked a little stern, but perhaps it was just her imagination. He certainly seemed to appreciate everything round him, except herself.

"I remember this room so well," he said. "The perfect symmetry of it has always made every other Dining-Room in which I have eaten seem ugly in comparison, and the picture over the mantelpiece has always been my favourite."

He looked at it as he went on:

"I used to stare at it as a little boy and imagine myself to be that Knight, so skilfully painted by Uccello, killing the dragon."

"It is difficult not to believe in dragons with the forest of Chinon just behind us," the *Comtesse* said, smiling.

"It used to seem very dark and mysterious to me," the Marquis said, "just as I am sure it would have seemed to any child."

He looked across the table at Yola.

"Did you imagine there were dragons when you went riding in the wood, Marie Teresa?" he asked. "And did the idea frighten you?"

He spoke in the mocking tone he had used to her when they had first met in the Winter Garden at the *Duc*'s house.

"I always imagined that the Knights who lived in the Castle would kill any dragons who might frighten me," Yola answered.

She looked appealingly at him as she spoke, hoping that he was really interested in her childhood dreams, but he merely turned to her grandmother to say:

"I imagine the sounds heard by the yokels and

ascribed to dragons were really the sounds of the wild boars. I expect there are still plenty of them to be hunted."

By the end of dinner, Yola, who had been unable to eat anything, was feeling as if she moved in a strange nightmare in which she was reaching out, trying to capture something that eluded her.

They moved back to the Salon, her grandmother again supported on the Marquis's arm.

They drank coffee and the Marquis accepted a glass of a well-matured brandy from the cellars, while the desultory conversation continued until Yola felt she would go mad.

It seemed as if a century passed before finally her grandmother rose to her feet.

"I have to retire early, Leonide," she said to the Marquis, "but I will leave you two young people to get to know each other. I am sure there are many things about the Castle which Marie Teresa can tell you better than anyone else."

"May I thank you once again for inviting me here," the Marquis replied.

He kissed the *Comtesse*'s hand, and opened the door for her to leave after she had said good-night to her granddaughter.

The Marquis shut the door and came back into the Salon. Yola, watching him advance, felt her tension leaving her.

They were alone, they were together! Now at last they could be themselves.

She waited for him to come to her and take her in his arms, but to her surprise he stopped at the coffee-table to pick up his glass of brandy.

"Your grandmother is a remarkable woman," he said conversationally. "She rather frightened me as a small boy, but even then I appreciated that she was very beautiful."

Yola looked at him in astonishment.

Surely now that they were alone he did not intend to continue this farce of pretending he did not recognise her?

"I hope tomorrow, Marie Teresa," he said, "you will not only show me the Castle, although I believe I could take myself round it blindfolded, but ride with me over the estate as I used to do with your father so many years ago."

"Leo!" Yola tried to say, but the word seemed to be strangled in her throat.

"I suppose," the Marquis continued, seating himself in an arm-chair, "that it is to be expected we should both feel somewhat awkward, knowing exactly what is required of us. So shall we dispense with all the unnecessary preliminaries?"

"Wh-what . . . do you . . . mean?"

Yola's question was hardly above a whisper.

She had not moved from where she was standing and now she put out her hand and held on to the back of a chair so that it would support her.

"I mean," the Marquis replied in that mocking voice she disliked, "we are both aware that we are to be married, so let me say without troubling to beat about the bush that I hope I will make you happy!"

For a moment Yola felt she could not have heard him aright.

Could he really be speaking to her in such a manner and in such words?

Could it really be Leo who was treating her as if her feelings were of no account and making it only too clear what he felt about her?

Before she could reply, he rose and walked to one of the windows, still holding his glass of brandy in his hand.

"This is one of the most perfect views in the world," he said, "but I suppose even a view would grow monotonous after a time. However, I am sure you and I will make the best of it, which is, after all, what your grandmother and father wished us to do."

Suddenly Yola gave a cry. It was like the sound of a small animal that has been hurt.

Then she rose and ran across the room to pull open the door of the Salon.

Without thinking what she was doing, she ran down the great staircase, out through the front door, across the court-yard, and along the terrace.

She did not choose where she was going—her feet just carried her away from the Castle, away from the Marquis, and when she stopped she found herself at the far end of the terrace where it turned to encircle the house.

In front of her was the view that the Marquis had admired from the Salon, but Yola could not see it for the tears that were gathering in her eyes.

She could only hold on to the stone balustrade and fight to stop herself from breaking down completely.

There was just a faint glow from the sun in the west but already the sky overhead was beginning to darken and the first evening stars were coming out.

The moon was but a shadow of itself but it was the same moon which had shone on them in the Bois when the Marquis had kissed her beside the cascade and she had known an ecstasy and a wonder that had carried her up to the Heavens.

Now she felt as if everything she had believed in, everything that was part of her father and her love, had been smashed and now lay round her in ruins.

The night was very still and there was only the sound of the birds going to roost.

Then she heard the Marquis's footsteps as he came from the court-yard onto the terrace.

He was a long way away and she contemplated wildly whether she would run down the steps which led to the second terrace, or, farther still, to the garden below.

Then she told herself that she would merely look foolish. What was the point of running away when he was staying in the Castle? She could not elude him forever.

He came nearer, moving without haste, leisurely at his ease, while she stood desperately holding on to the cold stone, staring out over the blossom-filled valley.

He reached her side, and she waited, her whole body stiff, for him to make some banal, commonplace remark in the tone he had used ever since he had arrived.

But he seemed to be in no hurry to speak and she knew his eyes were on her profile silhouetted against the darkening sky.

With an effort she forced herself to lift her chin a little proudly.

When finally he spoke, she thought his voice was stern and a little grim.

"Well, Marie Teresa Yola Lefleur de Beauharnais," he said, "what have you to say for yourself?"

It was hard to answer, but at last in a very small, low voice she asked:

"Are . . . you . . . angry?"

"Very!"

"I . . . I am . . . sorry."

He did not speak and she said in a whisper:

"H-have you . . . stopped . . . loving . . . me?"

"I am not concerned with *my* feelings at the moment," the Marquis answered, "but with your behaviour. How could you do anything so outrageous?"

"I . . . I had to . . . know the . . . truth about . . . you."

"Why?"

"B-because I thought . . . I could not . . . bear to . . . marry you."

"What had you heard about me, and from whom?"

"The girls at school used to . . . talk, and I overheard things from their parents. . . . I thought . . . you were the . . . type of man who would not be . . . happy at the C-Castle . . . and with . . . me."

"So you thought up that dangerous and reprehensible masquerade?"

"Y-yes."

He did not speak then, and despite every resolution Yola felt the tears begin to overflow from her eyes and run down her cheeks.

She did not move or wipe them away, hoping he would not see them. Then after a moment, because she could not bear the silence, she said in a broken little voice:

"I . . . I am sorry if it has . . . made you angry. Please . . . forgive me."

Again there was silence, and as if she could bear it no longer Yola turned towards him and hid her face against his shoulder.

"Forgive me . . . forgive me," she said as she sobbed. "I love you. Please . . . Leo . . . please . . . marry me."

He did not put his arms round her, and she felt frantically that he was unresponsive and that her happiness was slipping away from her and she would lose it completely.

"If you do not . . . love me enough to . . . marry me," she said, "let me be your . . . mistress, as you . . . asked me to be."

Her voice broke on the last words and now she was sobbing tempestuously, feeling she must collapse completely from the agony of the fear that she had lost him and he no longer wanted her.

At last the Marquis put his arms round her and held her against him. His action only made her cry the more.

"Are you quite sure that you love me?" he asked.

"I love you . . . desperately, agonisingly," Yola said as she wept. "I am yours! If you do not . . . want me anymore . . . if you do not love me . . . then all I want to do is . . . die!"

"My absurd, ridiculous darling."

Now the Marquis's voice was deep and tender. Yola stopped crying but her fingers clutched at the lapel of his coat.

He turned her face up to his and for a moment he looked at her, at the tears running down her cheeks, at her lips, soft and trembling.

Then his mouth came down on hers, and with a little sob that came from the very depths of her being she felt her happiness envelop her again, and the rapture he always aroused in her rose up from her breast to her lips.

She pressed herself nearer to him, wanting to melt into him, to be his completely. But, still holding her very closely, the Marquis raised his head to say:

"You still have a lot of explaining to do."

The severity of his words was belied by the gentleness in his voice.

"You are . . . not still . . . angry?"

"I ought to be. I am still appalled that you should have done anything so dangerous."

"I . . . thought I could . . . come home if . . . things got too . . . difficult."

"It might have been impossible."

She knew he was thinking of the moment when he had frightened her in the Café Anglais, and she hid her face again because the memory of it made her shy.

The Marquis read her thoughts.

"Exactly!" he said. "It was fortunate, my naughty one, that you were with me and not somebody else."

He felt Yola shiver and he went on:

"How could I have guessed, how could I have imagined, that anyone in your position would try to trick and deceive me by pretending to belong to a world about which you have no knowledge whatsoever?"

"I . . . deceived you . . . at first?"

"I was bewildered from the moment we met," the Marquis answered. "I knew that you were afraid, and that in itself was surprising. You were also inexperienced, unsophisticated, and, I finally discovered, very innocent."

He raised her face once again to his and looked down into her eyes.

"You are so lovely!" he said. "So incredibly, unbelievably beautiful, and when I realised who you were, I knew that nothing could stop me from marrying Marie Teresa de Beauharnais."

"You knew who I . . . was before . . . you arrived here!" Yola said accusingly. "Then . . . how could you have . . . acted so . . . cruelly?"

The Marquis smiled.

"I thought you deserved to be punished for taking such risks and not telling me the truth."

"I thought . . . you had . . . ceased to love me, and I thought the whole . . . world had fallen to pieces," Yola whispered.

"I wanted you to feel like that," the Marquis said. "At the same time, my precious, your punishment is not finished."

"Why not . . . if you will . . . marry me?"

"I intend to do that," the Marquis answered, "but you realise it will be a long time before you can return to Paris. If no-one else, the Prince Napoleon would recognise you."

"That does not worry me," Yola replied, "but will . . . you mind . . . very much?"

The Marquis smiled.

"I suppose I shall have to make the best of living in the most perfect Castle in the world and being married to a naughty, adorable wife who does the most unpredictable things."

"You . . . will be . . . happy here?"

"That of course remains to be seen," the Marquis answered.

As if he could not help himself, he kissed her forehead and then her eyes, and was seeking her mouth when Yola asked:

"Was it Aimée who told you who I was? If so, it was most disloyal of her."

"No, it was not Aimée," the Marquis replied, "and I am sure she would never have betrayed you. It was in fact the *Duc*."

"The *Duc*? But he did not know who I was."

"He had no idea," the Marquis agreed, "but after I had left you this morning, intending to catch the train at noon, I was suddenly afraid that the Prince Napoleon might make a nuisance of himself!"

"He did intend to . . . do so," Yola said in a low voice. "But go on!"

"I therefore drove to the *Duc*'s house in the Champs Élysées. I caught him just as he was going riding and I asked him if he would keep an eye on you and make sure that while I was away you did not go anywhere where you might encounter the Prince."

" 'You are going away?' the *Duc* questioned.

" 'I shall be back tomorrow,' I answered, 'but I have to visit Beauharnais Castle.'

" 'The most beautiful Castle in the Loire Valley,' the *Duc* said with a smile, 'and I miss Beauharnais. He was one of the nicest men I have ever known.'

" 'There I agree with you,' I replied. 'I miss him too.'

" 'He had a hell of a life with that tiresome wife,' the *Duc* said, 'but Gabrielle Renazé made him happy—very happy. I suppose you know she is Aimée's aunt?'

" 'Aimée's aunt?' I questioned. And in that moment I knew who you were!"

Yola made a little murmur but she did not interrupt.

"There had always been something about you which puzzled me," the Marquis went on. "There was something familiar in the way you carried yourself, something in your smile. And then I knew what it was: you were like your father, whom I had loved!"

"So that is how you found out!" Yola exclaimed.

"That is how I found out."

"And it . . . made you very . . . angry?"

"Very angry indeed to think that you should take such risks with yourself. Supposing . . . ?"

He stopped.

"What is the point of worrying about it?" he asked. "It is over. But I promise you, my precious, you will never again get the chance of doing anything so disgraceful. I shall keep you a prisoner here in the Castle and you will be chained to my side."

"That is . . . what I want," Yola replied. "I want to be with . . . you . . . always!"

She looked up at him and he saw the pleading expression in her eyes as she asked:

"This has not . . . spoilt our love? You still . . . love me?"

"More than anything else in the world."

"More than the . . . Castle?"

The Marquis smiled.

"I was prepared to give up the Castle for you, my precious one, but I cannot pretend I am not glad that it is still here for the two of us."

He turned her round as he spoke so that they could both look at it towering above them. The first gleam of moonlight was turning the towers to silver and glinting on the windows.

Gleaming in the dusk, against the starlit sky, it looked like a precious stone.

"Papa told you it was a . . . Castle made for . . . love," Yola whispered.

"And that is what we will make it," the Marquis said, "not only for ourselves, my sweetheart, but for those whom we must look after and help, as your father helped me."

Yola felt tears come into her eyes at the gratitude and affection in his voice. Then he drew her a little closer to him as he said:

"It must also, my darling, be a home of love for our children."

"I thought the . . . same thing. We must have . . . lots of children . . . they must never be lonely as I was."

"You will never be lonely again," the Marquis said positively. "I will love, protect, and look after you all my life!"

"That is all I want," Yola answered. "Oh, Leo, it really is a fairy-story come true! I have found you and you are everything Papa wanted you to be."

"And I have found my 'Sleeping Beauty,'" the Marquis answered. "It is going to take a whole lifetime to awaken her to the love that is not only part of a fairy-story but part of the glory of the Garden of France."

Yola thought of Saint Joan, and knew that once again she and the Marquis were attuned to each other's mind. They thought the same things and were already the other half of each other.

"I love you with all my heart," she said passionately, "and you must teach me all the things you want me to feel and to do. I want to love you as your wife and excite you as your mistress, but you must . . . show me how to do so."

The Marquis held her closer and there was a glint of fire in his eyes, but there was also an inexpressible tenderness.

"You already excite me, my adorable one," he said, "but my love for you is far greater than my desire for your exquisite body. I want so much more."

His lips were very close to Yola's as he said:

"I want your heart and your mind and your soul. I want to be sure that you are mine—mine completely and absolutely, with every breath you breathe and every thought you think."

"That is . . . what I . . . will give you," Yola whispered, "and together our love will fill the . . . whole world . . . yours and . . . mine."

"That is the love we have already," the Marquis said, "and what could be a more perfect place in which to keep it?"

He looked up for one moment at the Castle.

Then his mouth was on Yola's, holding her captive, drawing her closer and still closer to him.

She could feel his heart beating and knew that she excited him as she had wished to do.

At the same time, there was something sacred in the way he kissed her, a new reverence as she surrendered herself to the passionate, insistent demand of his lips.

Then she felt the wild, transcendent glory in them both, growing with the blossoms and the flowers, with the silver of the rivers and the starlight in the sky.

With the Castle, it enveloped and encircled them, giving them protection and also inspiration and strength, and a voice told Yola clearly that this was real love—the love which came from God.

ABOUT THE AUTHOR

BARBARA CARTLAND, the celebrated romantic author, historian, playwright, lecturer, political speaker and television personality, has now written over 150 books. Miss Cartland has had a number of historical books published and several biographical ones, including that of her brother, Major Ronald Cartland, who was the first Member of Parliament to be killed in the War. This book had a Foreword by Sir Winston Churchill.

In private life, Barbara Cartland, who is a Dame of the Order of St. John of Jerusalem, has fought for better conditions and salaries for Midwives and Nurses. As President of the Royal College of Midwives (Hertfordshire Branch), she has been invested with the first Badge of Office ever given in Great Britain, which was subscribed to by the Midwives themselves. She has also championed the cause for old people and founded the first Romany Gypsy Camp in the world.

Barbara Cartland is deeply interested in Vitamin Therapy and is President of the British National Association for Health.